THE NUMBERED MURDERS

A 1939 mystery

Peter Zander-Howell

Copyright © 2025 Peter Zander-Howell

All rights reserved.

Certain well-known historical persons are mentioned in this work. All other characters and events portrayed in this book are fictitious, and any similarity to real persons, alive or dead, is coincidental and not intended by the author. Real-world locations in this book may have been slightly altered.

No part of this book may be reproduced, or stored in a retrieval system, or transmitted in any form or by any means, electronic, mechanical, photocopying, recording, or otherwise, without the express permission of the publisher.

ISBN - 9798311843461

PREFACE

In July 1939, three men are shot dead within a few days of each other. The incidents are all in Lancashire but in different police force areas.

When it is eventually realised that the cases are linked, the various constabularies agree to call in the expertise of Scotland Yard. Detective Chief Inspector Adair, who has been holidaying with his wife and daughter in the same county, is tasked with investigating the crimes.

These do not appear to be random shootings. It seems that the gunman has a motive for killing each of the victims. But what could that be? And is the grudge against each one as an independent individual, or are the victims themselves linked in some way?

CONTENTS

Title Page
Copyright
Preface

CHAPTER 1	1
CHAPTER 2	15
CHAPTER 3	23
CHAPTER 5	29
CHAPTER 6	34
CHAPTER 7	44
CHAPTER 8	49
CHAPTER 9	59
CHAPTER 10	65
CHAPTER 11	75
CHAPTER 12	86
CHAPTER 13	93
CHAPTER 14	100
CHAPTER 15	112
CHAPTER 16	122

CHAPTER 17	135
CHAPTER 18	151
CHAPTER 19	162
Books By This Author	171

CHAPTER 1

On a dry and comfortably warm July Sunday in 1939, Muriel Cavanagh was working at her kitchen sink. Through the window, she saw the family's English setter run into the garden through the open back gate. Assuming that Tess had simply run ahead of her master who had taken her for a walk in the nearby woods, Muriel resumed her task, but seconds later the dog reached the back door and started to bark. This was unprecedented, and the Lancashire housewife quickly dried her hands and went to open the door. The dog didn't come in, but just stood on the doorstep looking up at her and whining.

Muriel realised that something was wrong. Perhaps Aiden had fallen and broken his leg? But even as that thought flashed across her mind in the seconds she stood at the door, it was pushed aside by a far worse one. Had he had a heart attack and was lying dead?

It took her only a few more seconds to decide what to do. She and Aiden lived by themselves now, their daughter and two sons having flown the nest – the youngest only a matter of weeks ago when he followed the examples of his older siblings and got married.

Muriel tore off her apron and ran out of the front door. Without her noticing, Tess followed, no longer whining.

The houses were detached, in a largely middle-class village. Her neighbour on one side was a widower in his seventies. On the other side was Stuart Handley, a general surgeon from the hospital in the nearby town, and Muriel ran some twenty yards along the road to his gate. She banged frantically on the front door, praying that he would be at home.

The door was opened by his wife, Alexandra, who immediately realised that something was wrong. Before she could speak, Muriel blurted out, "Oh Alex, is Stu in? Aiden is missing."

In fact, Stuart heard this, having been on his way to the front door himself, and appeared behind his wife.

"What's happened, Mu? Come in anyway."

Muriel shook her head, and quickly explained what had happened. "Would you go and look for him, Stu? I daren't. You know Tess, and I feel sure she'll show you the way."

"Of course, Mu. She's followed you here, I see. I'll just collect Eliot, and we'll see where Tess takes us. Don't worry – Aiden's probably just fallen over and broken a leg. Come inside, and Alex will get you a drink."

Eliot, the Handley's only son, was home from university, and came down to his father's shout up the stairs. As Alexandra shepherded Muriel into the lounge, Stuart put his son in the picture. Tess sat patiently in the hall.

The two men went out via the back door, the dog following without being called.

At their back gate, Tess moved into the lead, and trotted along the path around the edge of a field, clearly aiming for the woods a quarter of a mile away. Every fifty or so yards, she stopped and turned to check that the men were still following.

"She's a clever girl," remarked Eliot.

"Brighter than many a human," agreed his father.

The dog entered the wood, and trotted along a path which both Handleys knew well from their own perambulations. They were deep in the wood, when Tess, in the lead by some twenty yards, suddenly stopped and let out a single bark. She then lay down, looking at something ahead.

The men, on reaching her, saw at once what she was staring at. A man, obviously Aiden Cavanagh, was lying on the ground a few yards away. He was on his back, and didn't move.

Handley put his arm out to stop his son.

"Stay there," he instructed. He then moved to within a few feet of his friend, looking down. He stayed in this position for half a minute, without making any attempt to touch the man. He then spoke without turning around.

"Eliot, get back home as fast as you can. Telephone for an ambulance, and for the police. Say that Aiden Cavanagh has been shot dead. And Eliot – emphasise to the police that this isn't a shotgun accident. It looks to me as though he's been hit in the chest by a single bullet. I'll stay here with the body."

"Oh Lord, Dad, this is awful. Could it be suicide?"

"No, I don't think so. First of all it's very hard to shoot oneself in the chest with a handgun. In the temple, or through the roof of the mouth are more usual places. Even harder with a rifle – but I'm sure that cartridge casing isn't from a rifle. Anyway, I don't see a gun."

Eliot turned to go, but had only just started to run when his father called him back.

"No; stop. I'll have to go – I have experience at breaking bad news to a spouse. You stay on guard. But I must emphasise, don't go any closer. If, as I suspect, this is murder, the last thing the police want is a load of footsteps trampling all round the body. Will you be all right?"

"Well, this is the first time I've seen a dead body, Dad, but I'm okay."

The surgeon reached down to pat Tess, and then turned to go back. He guessed, correctly, that the dog would choose to remain with her master.

Handley entered his house quietly, slipped into his study and closed the solid door. He picked up the telephone. His first call was to the town police station, where he spoke to a sergeant. This officer undertook to contact someone in the CID as soon as possible. After hanging up, Handley changed his mind about calling for an ambulance next, and called a local doctor instead.

"Tim – Stuart Handley here. Listen, are you still the local Police Surgeon? Good. Now, it's not for me to give you work, but my neighbour has just been shot dead, and I suspect foul play. I've called the police, but you are definitely going to be needed. Could you come round to my house right away? Thanks, old chap."

The surgeon paused for a moment to collect himself, and then left the study and went into the lounge.

Muriel rose from her chair as he came in, and immediately saw from his face that the news was going to be the worst.

"Oh God, Stu – is Aiden dead?"

She started to cry before Handley could even answer, and collapsed back into the chair.

He nodded sadly. "I'm very sorry to say that he is, Mu. It was very quick."

He indicated that his wife should come out into the hall. There he spoke quietly. "Alex, Aiden was shot – I think murdered. I've called the police and the Police Surgeon. I suggest you take Mu home. Call Fiona and Danny if you can get them, and see if one or both can come straight away to join their mother. Maybe also call Jim Ferris, he's their GP – he could give her something. I must go back and take over from Eliot. I'll send him back here. When the police or Tim Curtis arrive, he can show them where to go. Aiden is in a clearing in the middle of Claydon Wood."

Mrs Handley had looked shocked when her husband mentioned murder, but hadn't spoken. Now she just whispered "Why, for God's sake?"

The question being rhetorical, the surgeon shrugged, and turned to go.

In the clearing, he found Eliot sitting on a fallen tree trunk, with Tess beside him.

"Has anybody else come by?"

"No, Dad; not a soul."

"All right. I've called the police, and also the police surgeon. You've met Tim Curtis, I think. I have no idea how long they'll be, but Tim is quite close, and will probably arrive first.

"Go back home, and bring him or the police back here. I've broken the news to Muriel, and Mum is taking her home and will try to contact their offspring."

"Poor Mu," muttered Eliot, taking one last look at the body before turning to leave.

Handley took his son's place on the convenient tree trunk, and almost absent-mindedly started to rub the setter's ears.

He stared at the body for a long time, contemplating the small brass object lying on the chest close to the wound.

Ten minutes later, he heard the sound of voices, and shortly afterwards his son returned to the glade, accompanied by Doctor Curtis. Handley stood.

"'Morning Tim," he said, shaking hands. "My next-door neighbour, Aiden Cavanagh," he indicated with a gesture towards the body.

"Eliot, you'd better go back to the house and wait for the police."

Doctor Curtis, who like Handley earlier had remained a few feet from the body looking at it intently, now turned away.

"Well, as you obviously decided yourself, Stu, I don't need to get out a stethoscope. And although a post mortem will be necessary, I don't anticipate any surprises there. Shot with a large calibre weapon, and the cartridge case is lying here. From what you say, the time of death is known more accurately than I could estimate it, so I'll wait for the police before poking around any more."

The two doctors sat on the fallen tree. Curtis pulled out a packet of cigarettes, and offered one to his colleague. Handley, who normally smoked a pipe, accepted. They sat quietly, occasionally exchanging a sentence or two. Tess lay down by the men's feet.

After nearly half an hour, the sound of voices reached them, and a minute later Eliot appeared again, leading two men in suits. He stepped aside, and the senior detective, a tall man in his mid-forties, moved forward.

"'Morning Doc, hello Stuart," said Inspector

Wainwright. "This is Sergeant Ellison. He jerked a thumb towards his colleague, an even taller man who might have just reached the age of thirty.

"Ellison, this is Mr Handley – I play golf with him sometimes – and he took my appendix out a year or two ago! You know Doctor Curtis, of course."

The policemen stood looking down at the body, in just the same way that the two doctors had.

"Nasty business, then," muttered Wainwright over his shoulder.

"I've waited for you to come before I take a closer look, Inspector, but we know the time of death."

"Thanks, Doc. We'll just bag up the casing that I see here, and then you can carry on. Did you call for an ambulance, Stu?"

"No, John. I didn't know how long you would need on site, so I didn't want the crew having to stand around for hours."

"Won't be very long. We can move the body as soon as the Doc's finished. Perhaps your son could go and do the necessary?"

Eliot nodded, and was about to set off for the house once again when his father stopped him.

"Take the ambulance men around past Littlejohn's house, Eliot – Muriel might see a stretcher coming through our house to get to the road, and we don't want that."

"What can you tell us about today – and

about the deceased?" asked Wainwright after Eliot had gone.

"About today, very little," replied Handley. Muriel – Aiden's wife – came banging on our door at ten past eleven. Tess here had come home without Aiden, and apparently made it clear that something was wrong. So Eliot and I came this way – the dog leading us.

"I've known Aiden for about seven years – we both moved into our respective houses on the same day. He and I have become good friends, as have Alex and Muriel. Aiden doesn't play golf, but we dine in each other's houses at least once a month, usually with whist to follow. The two of us have a drink in the Fox at least once, most weeks.

"He's a business man – owns a couple of factories. I gather a hundred or so people are employed in each. One is a cotton mill, and the other makes metal instruments of various sorts. I think both are doing very well. Not sure what else I can tell you. He's a sociable sort of chap, gets on with all the locals in the pub, and so on. But no doubt you'll be looking to find someone he's sacked."

"Yes, I suppose so. We're assuming that he was targeted, of course, and that this wasn't either an accident or a random murder by some deranged individual."

Curtis had got up from the body, and now he and the Sergeant joined the others.

"Which do you reckon is easier for you,

Inspector – a random murderer with no motive, or someone with a specific grudge?"

"To tell the truth, Doc, I have no experience in murder cases at all. We in the County police don't see many, as you know. But I suppose it might be better to be able to look through a load of people who knew the victim, and try to find one with a motive. And the means," he added.

"Don't want to say anything out of line, sir," said Ellison, speaking for the first time, "but could there be a possibility that Mr Cavanagh was having an affair with a married woman, and a husband took exception to it?"

There was a silence for a few seconds.

"I grant you that could be a possibility, Sergeant," said Handley at last. "All I can say is I never saw the slightest indication that Aiden was given to philandering. But if he was, I suppose you also have to consider that Muriel might have found out, and killed him herself. And that I simply can't believe."

"I'm off," announced Curtis. "Nothing more I can do here. If you get him to the hospital mortuary, Inspector, I'll do the *post mortem* this afternoon."

He raised a hand in salute, and turned away.

"How did Mrs Cavanagh take the news, Stu?" asked Wainwright.

"Tears; she was very upset, naturally. But I think she'll be pretty stoic when you interview her, as I suppose you must. Actually I suggested that

Alex should call their GP – if he's been then he may well have given Muriel a sedative."

Wainwright was about to reply when Tess suddenly stood up and turned towards the path going deeper into the wood. A few seconds later she let out a single growl as a middle-aged man and woman came into the clearing. They were followed by a black Labrador retriever. Tess moved to stand between the newcomers and the body, and the two detectives joined her.

"Hello, Tess, what's the matter girl?" asked the man as he drew near, "you always come for a pat. Where's her master?" he asked the two men standing by the dog. His own dog approached her friend Tess, tail wagging. The setter growled, and the retriever backed off and sat down – looking almost surprised, Wainwright thought.

Before either officer could answer the question, the man and woman noticed Handley by the fallen tree.

"Hello, Stuart," called the woman, "what's going on?"

Handley moved closer.

"Sad news, I'm afraid. Aiden is dead. Inspector Wainwright and his colleague here are detectives."

The Sergeant moved aside slightly, and both newcomers saw the body.

"Oh Lord," exclaimed the woman, swaying against her husband.

"Detectives?" enquired the man. "You mean

there's been foul play?"

"Alas, yes, Dermot," replied Handley. "Sorry, John – this is Alicia and Dermot Howarth. They also live in the village."

"I have to ask a couple of questions, sir and madam," said Wainwright.

"First, your address, if you please."

Alicia supplied this, and Ellison wrote it down.

"Thank you. Now, during your walk today, did you walk through this clearing before?"

Howarth shook his head. "No; we came into the wood from the other side. Then we go through and back home past Handley's and Cavanagh's houses. Sometimes we reverse that route, for a change as it were."

"Have you seen anyone else this morning?"

"Not a soul," replied Alicia. "Well, we saw two boys playing on their bicycles in the road near our house, but nobody after we left the road and set off around the field."

"Did you hear a gunshot, within the last couple of hours?"

"No," both Howarths spoke together. "We do occasionally hear shooting, the local landowner and his gamekeeper, you know, but it would be very noticeable on a Sunday," added Dermot. "I assume you're saying Aiden was shot?"

"Correct, sir – but the sound of this shot would be rather different to that from a shotgun – a pistol rather than a twelve-bore or four-ten. And

I suppose that deep in these woods, with all the trees in leaf, the sound might not travel far."

"Oh God – not a shooting accident, then."

"No. These boys you saw – do you know them"

"Oh yes, Inspector, they both live in the village," answered Alicia. "David Markham and Dai Pryce-Jones. Nice lads, both twelve or thirteen, I should think. Dai's father is landlord of the local public house, the Fox and Hounds. David's father is the blacksmith, and has recently taken to selling petrol and doing some basic car maintenance and so on."

Wainwright glanced at Ellison, who was scribbling in his pocketbook. "Got all that, Sergeant?"

"Yes, sir."

"We may need to come and talk to you again, but that's all for now; thank you."

After the Howarths had gone, Wainwright looked at the body again, and then seemed to come to a decision.

"The ambulance shouldn't be too long now, but I need to speak to the widow as soon as possible. Stuart, would you come back with me and introduce me to Mrs Cavanagh? You stay here, Ellison. Tell the ambulance boys to get the body to the hospital morgue, and when they've done that come and find me next door to Mr Handley's.

"Will the dog come back with you, Stu? If she stays here I can see her getting annoyed if a couple of strangers arrive and start moving her late master."

"I sometimes take her for a walk myself – so does my son, actually. She's normally very obedient, and comes if I call her, but her behaviour today has been very unusual – quite understandable, of course. She'll probably come with us. A pity she can't speak, as presumably she could identify the killer."

The two men turned towards the exit path. "Come on, Tess," called the surgeon. Almost reluctantly it seemed, the setter rose to her feet, looked once more at the body of her master, and obediently followed.

CHAPTER 2

When they reached the rear of the properties, Handley took the inspector through the Cavanaghs' gate and tapped on the back door. The door was opened by a young woman, who gave Handley a wan little smile.

"Hello, Stuart; please don't say the conventional things – that seems to make it worse rather than better. Come inside. You'll be a police officer, no doubt?" she added, looking at the other man.

"Yes, Fee, this is Detective Inspector Wainwright – someone Alex and I have known for years. John, this is Aiden's daughter, Fiona Abbott.

"How is your mother bearing up, Fee?"

"She seems to be taking it as well as could be expected. I've only been here about ten minutes – Danny is with her now, and Alex is here too. I gather Doctor Ferris called a little while ago and gave her a powder. Come through – she's expecting to have to answer questions."

Fiona led the two men into the main living room, and Tess followed. Muriel was seated in the centre of a large settee, with Alex Handley on one side and a young man on the other. The man rose to his feet, and Fiona performed the introductions.

"Mum, Danny, this is Detective Inspector Wainwright; Inspector, my mother and my brother Daniel. I understand you know Mr Wainwright already, Alex."

Without rising, Muriel Cavanagh extended her hand, and Wainwright leaned down to shake it. As he did so, she spoke.

"Do please find a seat, Inspector, and dispense with the conventional sympathies. Aiden has been murdered, and I'm looking to you to find the man who did this, so he can be hanged. I'm not in the mood for forgiveness right now, and I don't think I ever shall be."

Handley intervened before Wainwright could respond.

"You have Fee and Danny here now, Mu – I suggest Alex and I leave you with your family and the Inspector."

"Bless you for coming back with me and getting hold of the children, Alex. Both of you, please come and see me again this evening."

As Alex rose from the settee, Tess jumped up, and took her place. Her mistress patted the dog gently. "What a clever dog you are, Tess."

She looked at Wainwright, now seated in an armchair opposite. "I have never seen Tess jump up on the furniture before. It's almost uncanny – she just knows the situation.

"We were just thinking about having a cup of coffee, Inspector – no doubt you'd like one?"

"Very kind, ma'am."

"Fee, Danny, would you sort that between you, please. Mr Wainwright and I will have a quiet chat while you two are in the kitchen."

As soon as the others had left the room, Muriel looked hard at the Inspector.

"Please give me the blunt facts. How was my husband killed?"

"He was shot through the heart with a single bullet from a pistol, ma'am. He would have died instantly."

Muriel was silent for a moment.

"What will happen now? I assume it's best that I don't see him yet."

"My Sergeant is guarding him at present. An ambulance will come shortly, and take him away. By law there will have to be a *post mortem* examination. That will be conducted by Doctor Curtis, who attended at the scene just now. The Coroner will convene an inquest within the next day or so, but it's likely he will adjourn that to give the police time to make enquiries. I'm afraid I can't tell you how long it will be before you can arrange the funeral. The Coroner's Officer will contact you."

"I see; thank you. You want to ask me about anyone who might have disliked Aiden enough to kill him. Well, the answer is that I have no idea. We live quietly enough here, and get on with everyone we know in the village – which after seven years here is practically everyone. Stuart will have told you that Aiden owns two factories. One is a limited company, and he is chairman and majority shareholder. The other is a private company. Aiden is very much involved in policy decisions, but for two or three years now he hasn't involved himself in the day to day running. Each factory is *de facto* run by a manager, and each manager has a deputy.

"So, if you are thinking that he sacked some employee, and that individual then killed him in revenge, I just don't believe that's likely. But of course you'll want to talk to the managers and others.

"Incidentally, although a number of workers had to be laid off in the depths of the Depression, for the last couple of years both factories have been working flat out, and there is work for all.

"Nearer to home, there just isn't anyone. We have a few close friends – like Alex and Stuart – with whom we socialise. And Aiden would go for a drink in the Fox once or twice a week, and sometimes have a game of crib or darts. There has never, to my knowledge, been any sort of disagreement or unpleasantness there – but again, you can talk to the landlord, a charming little Welshman."

Fiona and Danny returned, each carrying a tray. The conversation was paused while Fiona poured the coffee.

"I've been telling the Inspector about your

father's businesses," resumed Muriel, and why I can't think this could be the work of a disgruntled employee or ex-employee."

"That's logical, Inspector," agreed Daniel. "Mother, Fee, our brother Richard and I are all directors. But we only deal with major decisions on policy and direction – never on day-to-day operational matters. So if Knipe, for example – he's the managing director of Cavanagh & Company – or one of his supervisors sacked somebody, we on the board would be unlikely even to hear about it. Same for Rigge at Lancashire Metal Holdings."

"Understood, Mr Cavanagh. Nevertheless, we have to start looking somewhere. Perhaps you would write down the names and addresses of the factories, and the names of the managers and their immediate deputies?"

"Of course." Danny stood up and left the room.

"Dad was such a pleasant man," remarked Fiona, who looked to be nearer to tears than her mother. "He was so unlike the popular image of a mill owner – you know, someone who grinds the faces of the poor in the dirt. He set up welfare provisions and so on – one of the few in his position to do that, I think. About ten years ago there was an accident in the mill one day. One of the men lost an arm, which meant he couldn't continue in his job. I was a child, and didn't know anything about it at the time. But I've since learned that father found him a job as a night watchman in another firm – and is still paying him a pension to bring his earnings up to what it was as a skilled mill operative.

"You'll be hard-pressed to find anyone in the factories wanting to murder him."

Wainwright nodded slowly. "Yet the fact remains that someone, for some reason, did."

"What about mistaken identity, Inspector?" enquired Muriel.

"Still possible, of course, ma'am. But this was done in a lonely spot, with nobody else around. The murderer seems to have known that his victim would be coming that way. If in fact the target was somebody else, that would mean that another of the presumably very few people who use that path was the intended victim – almost certainly someone else in this village. Is there some reviled local who would fit that bill?"

Both women slowly shook their heads.

"Another possibility is that this was a random killing by some madman. But although there are no doubt many pistols in private hands – some owned legally and others not – one hopes not too many are held by homicidal maniacs. If this is such a case, I fear there will be further killings."

Daniel returned, and handed the Inspector a sheet of paper. "I've included the telephone numbers for the managers – being Sunday they may be at home, but both factories are currently operating seven days a week, so it's possible they'll be at work."

"Anyway, ma'am," continued Wainwright after draining the last of his coffee and standing up, "I won't trespass any more on your time. I assure you all that we'll do our best to find this man quickly."

"You're assuming it's a man, Inspector," called Muriel as he reached the door. "But surely a woman could use a pistol just as well?"

"Quite true, ma'am," replied Wainwright, turning back to face her, "and we'll certainly bear the possibility in mind. But I can't recall ever hearing of a female committing murder by shooting – poison is their more usual method, I believe."

Fiona let the Inspector out through the front door, and he returned to the car. There was no sign of Ellison, but a hundred yards further along he could see an ambulance. He got in the car and reversed along the lane to park behind it.

As he got out of the car again, both Handleys appeared, leading two ambulance men bearing a blanket-covered stretcher. Sergeant Ellison brought up the rear.

All four men stood with bowed heads as the crew loaded the body into their vehicle.

"Good hunting, John," said Handley as the policemen got into their car.

"Hell of a job, Stu," replied Wainwright. "Nothing to go on as yet. I'll see you again soon, hopefully in more pleasant circumstances.

"Drive to the local station first Ellison – we'll

see if they can give us a room to work in. Then we'll work out how we're going to interview the factory managers, and probably most of the adults in the village."

CHAPTER 3

Three days later, no progress had been made in the investigation. At a little after six o'clock, on the Wednesday evening, while Inspector Wainwright was in the Fox and Hounds talking for the second time to Aled Pryce-Jones and his son Dai, another murder was being committed thirty miles away.

Like Aiden Cavanagh on Sunday, Paul Hargreaves was out for a walk. He was unaccompanied, having neither wife nor dog. He scarcely ever altered his routine, and during the summer months followed the same route on at least three evenings each week. (Between October and April, when it was too dark to do this after work, he changed to an all-road itinerary.)

On this day, however, he too entered a wood a few hundred yards from his home – and never emerged. A pair of lovers sauntering through the wood found the body about an hour later.

The young swain, Alan Sims, bent over the body and despite his lack of medical knowledge realised at once that the man was dead, and announced this to his *inamorata*, Daisy Bolton.

Daisy, who had hung back on seeing the body, promptly dived into the bushes, retching.

"Sorry, Al," she said on recovering. "I've never seen a dead person before. Do you know who it is?"

"I think I might have seen him around sometime, but I don't know him. Anyway, we must go and call for help."

The two young people, their outing ruined, made their way back to the populated roads and found a telephone kiosk. Sims wasn't sure which emergency service he should ask for, but eventually opted for the police. He made his report about the body, described the location as best he could, and gave his own name and address. The officer taking the details didn't ask him to stay where he was, so he and Daisy wandered off again – but didn't go back to the woods.

Half an hour later, Constable Rose arrived on his bicycle. He was familiar with the area, and the directions from Sims had been accurate. When he had pedalled as far as he could, he then pushed his bicycle further along the path. Reaching the body, he leaned his machine against a tree. Although still daylight, within the wood it was getting darker, and Rose removed his bicycle lantern to get a better look. He squatted down beside the body.

In the absence of any visible indications, Rose made the not-unreasonable assumption that the man had suffered a heart attack. He noticed a brass cartridge case lying in the leaf mould beside the body. Without thinking – and Rose wasn't the quickest thinker anyway – he picked this up and slipped it in his pocket.

He then cycled back, and went to the same telephone kiosk that Sims had used earlier. The first question his superior at the police station asked was whether the body was situated within the boundary of the Borough. Rose confirmed that it was – just. The Sergeant said that he would arrange for an ambulance, and told Rose to wait where he was in order to show the crew where to go. There was no suggestion of fetching a doctor.

By the time another half hour had passed, the body had been removed to the local mortuary, and Rose, in the absence of any other instructions, had returned to his station. The Desk Sergeant simply told him to write up a statement, and said that a local doctor would look at the body in the morning.

The constabulary didn't run to an appointed police surgeon – and recently on the rare occasions that the police wanted a vaguely professional assessment as to whether a person was or was not drunk, they called on Andrew Marshall, a young general practitioner. In fact it was nearly noon the next day before Dr Marshall was persuaded to look at the body and find the cause of death.

Marshall had attended three *post mortem* examinations during his training some ten years before, but had never been called upon to carry one out himself. Reluctantly, he went to the town mortuary. The attendant indicated the relevant corpse, and the two men lifted it onto a marble slab, which the man said hadn't been used in the twelve years he had worked in the place.

"Let's get his clothes off," said the doctor.

During this process, the dead man's back was exposed, and both men immediately saw the cause of death.

"Shot in the back, Blenkinsop. No scorch marks or anything like that, so not done at very close range. Oh Lord. Although he doesn't seem to have bled much, surely there must have been blood on the stretcher when they lifted him off in here? How did they miss it?

"Oh well, I'd better dig out the bullet. It clearly went through his heart and into his sternum."

Marshall had borrowed an old case of surgical instruments from a colleague whose deceased father had been a surgeon, rightly assuming that modern sterile equipment wouldn't be needed, and that a couple of scalpels and a saw would probably suffice anyway.

He started as he had seen his old pathology tutor do years ago, and started to open the torso from collar bone to pelvis.

Twenty minutes later, Marshall stepped back from the corpse, stripped off his gloves, and went to the sink to wash his hands under the single cold tap. The out-of-shape bullet, now wrapped in cotton wool, was sitting in a small glass jar. Other jars contained various bodily parts.

"I don't suppose there will be any need to get those organs analysed for poison or anything, but they'll be available if the Coroner wants it done.

"Sew him up as best you can, please Blenkinsop. Do we know who he is, by the way? I feel I've seen him somewhere before."

"No name on him, Doc. Found in Barton Woods last night, apparently."

"All right. I'll go and contact the police and inform the Coroner."

There being no telephone in the mortuary, Marshall drove back to his surgery. It didn't take long to transmit his findings to the police – and the Desk Sergeant to whom he spoke undertook to pass the information up the chain immediately.

The part-time Coroner for the Borough was a local solicitor, and Marshall telephoned his firm. It seemed that Mr Firbank was sitting at his desk having a sandwich, and had no client with him. The call was put through. The Coroner took the details, and on being told that the identity of the murdered man was unknown, asked for his approximate age, a rough description, and the location of where he was found.

That provided, there was a short silence before Mr Firbank spoke again.

"My partner, Paul Hargreaves, hasn't turned up today, Doctor, and hasn't telephoned to explain. He's missed a couple of appointments. He's a widower, living alone – doesn't even have any live-in servants. I was just sitting here thinking about sending one of our clerks to call and see if he is ill.

"Your description could fit him. And he lives very close to the Barton Woods. I'd better see if I can identify him. Is he in the Stockley Street mortuary?"

"Yes, sir – and the attendant Blenkinsop was there when I left twenty minutes ago. I don't know if he's on duty all day, but I gave him the job of stitching up the body, so I guess he'll be there for a while yet to let you in."

"Good. I'll go immediately. If, Heaven forbid, it is Hargreaves, I'll inform the police. Thank you, Doctor. Let the police have your PM report – don't send it to me direct."

CHAPTER 5

Within half an hour of this telephone conversation, Firbank was back in his office. Picking up the telephone, he asked for the police station, and when finally connected he identified himself to the Desk Sergeant.

"The body you have in the morgue, Sergeant – I understand Doctor Marshall has told you he was shot?"

"That's right, sir. For some reason that fact wasn't noted by those on the scene."

"No, well I'm not concerned with that at present. I'm calling to tell you who the man is. I've just been to view the body, and it is Paul Hargreaves, my partner in Firbank and Hargreaves. You need to pass that on to whoever is investigating what seems to be a case of murder."

When the Coroner ended the call, Sergeant Bailey left his desk and walked a few yards along a corridor to what the little constabulary was pleased to call the 'CID Office'. The plain clothes section of the force consisted of only two men – a sergeant and a constable. Inside the room, a clearly angry Detective Sergeant Adams was talking to three men standing in front of his desk.

One was Constable Rose, and the others were the ambulance men who had transported the body to the mortuary. (The ambulance service in the Borough came under the jurisdiction of the Chief Constable.)

"I suppose there's some excuse for you, Rose, in that the man was face up and you couldn't see that he had been shot in the back. But you two – my God, if you didn't see what had happened when you lifted him onto the stretcher, surely there must have been blood left on the surface of the stretcher when you lifted him off in the morgue?"

"Not really, Sarge," protested the older of the ambulance men. We had a double layer of sheet on the stretcher, lifted the body onto it, and wrapped it in the rest of the sheets. A sort of shroud, like. When we took the body into the morgue, we just lifted it, sheet and all. We never unwrapped him. I'll swear there was no blood on the stretcher."

Adams grunted, somewhat mollified. This state lasted only a few seconds, because Rose now came out with something else. Fishing in his pocket, he produced the brass cartridge case he had taken from the scene. He silently laid this on Adams' desk.

Adams stared at it for some moments.

"You two get out," he instructed the ambulance men.

"You'd better explain, Rose."

The hapless constable began to stutter.

"I just saw it there near the body, Sarge. Just picked it up, sort of automatically. Was going to give it to my little grandson. Never thought the man had been shot you see, so didn't have any reason to think it was important."

"You see large calibre pistol cartridge cases lying around in the woods quite often, do you? You didn't ask yourself what it was doing there? Well, if there was any chance of getting a print off this one I guess that's gone. I suppose the only thing remotely in your favour is that you've belatedly come clean about it. Get out of my sight now. Write up your statement."

When Rose had gone, Adams looked at his colleague Bailey.

"We've not got off to a good start on this one, Jimmy. But I can see you haven't come in here for a chat. What is it?"

"We've just got a name for the dead man. Paul Hargreaves, a solicitor – and partner of our Coroner, who has just been to identify the body. He's given us the man's home address, too. And twenty minutes ago Doc Marshall brought in the contents of the dead man's pockets. Until Mr Firbank called there was nothing to identify him – he wasn't wearing a jacket and there was no wallet or anything. But there were some keys."

He pushed a note and a bunch of keys to his colleague.

"Well, that's a start," said Adams. "To be

frank, I have no real idea how to tackle this. We haven't had a murder in the Borough this century. The Super is hopping, and he's trying to find the Chief – nobody seems to know where he is today. I've lost DC Briggs myself – he went out before the Doc told us the man was shot, and I can't contact him.

"Still, I can go and search this house now, talk to neighbours and so on. You heard the farce about the brass casing – for all I know there might have been a pistol on site that Rose didn't see. We'll have to search there as well. Anyway, thanks for the info, Jimmy.

"If DC Briggs comes in, please tell him from me to go and do a fingertip search on the ground and in any bushes near where the body was found. If Rose is still in the station, can you spare him to show Briggs the spot?"

"Sure – unless I've had to send him out somewhere else. If I see the Super – or the Chief – I'll pass on the name of the deceased."

"Thanks. When the brass hears that he was a solicitor and the Coroner's partner, I rather think there's going to be a lot of interference in this investigation!"

***

Word of Cavanagh's murder spread quite fast around his village. However, there was no 'stringer' for the local newspaper, and at the time Adams and Bailey were talking, knowledge of that killing had not yet reached the Press. As it had occurred in a constabulary other than their own, news hadn't spread to their station through any police grapevine either.

The following day, that absence of communication would change.

CHAPTER 6

On Friday morning, in another Lancashire town, Frank Gould was working in the garden of his big detached house. Gould, a sixty-year-old recently-retired banker, saw a taxicab draw up by the front gate. He was expecting the car, as his wife Miriam had told him over breakfast that she was going on a shopping expedition, one which he was not expected to attend. Indeed, seconds later Miriam emerged from the house, and approached within calling range.

"I'm off, dear. I'm having lunch with Emmeline Deacon, so I won't be back until about four o' clock. You'll have to find something to eat yourself – a call came from a neighbour of Annie's mother, to say she is very poorly and asking if Annie can get over there quickly. Naturally I said Annie could go, and gave her money for the return train fare to Newcastle. She left to go to the station a few minutes ago.

"And Mary has Fridays off, of course. She went out as soon as breakfast was cleared away. You're on your own."

"All right, my dear; I'll manage somehow. See you later – no doubt I'll hardly recognise you under the pile of parcels you'll be carrying!"

The day was already quite warm, and Gould had been active, pushing the Panther hand mower up and down the front lawn. He decided to go back into the house for a glass of something cold. Five past eleven in the morning was perhaps a little early for a beer, he thought, but Annie had made some lemonade the day before, and he thought there might be some left in a jug in the pantry. He abandoned the roller mower, and went inside to investigate.

Ten minutes later, he was sitting in his drawing room reading his Manchester Guardian, with a glass of lemonade on the little table beside him.

The front door bell jangled loudly. For a few seconds Gould ignored it, before realising that he was the only person in the house and would have to go to the door himself. Putting down his newspaper, he got up and went to the front door.

Facing him on the step was a well-dressed man, who said that he had heard Gould was Chairman of the local Conservative Association, and asked if he could discuss standing in the next county council elections.

Gould, always on the lookout for good candidates, knew that a vacancy would soon arise. He at once invited the man inside. After closing the front door, Gould started to lead the visitor to the drawing room before remembering that there was no more lemonade to offer. He altered course for the study instead.

In the study, Gould walked a few feet into the room, and then turned around preparatory to shaking hands and learning the name of his visitor.

In the second of his life remaining, he realised the man had remained in the doorway and was now pointing a gun at him. The shot was very loud within the room, but would not have been audible outside the house – even if there had been neighbours close by.

The killer left the house only two minutes after he had arrived, and walked off unhurriedly down the lane. There was nobody about, and two hundred yards later he joined a more populated road, where various pedestrians and motorists were passing. Nobody took any particular notice of the man.

***

Miriam Gould returned home a little after four o'clock, as promised. As her husband had forecast, she had a number of bags and parcels, which the taxi driver helped to carry into the house. After he had been paid, Mrs Gould first went to divest herself of her hat, and change into slightly less formal attire. She then went to the kitchen, where she made a pot of tea.

Pouring two cups, she carried these into

the drawing room, where she saw the abandoned newspaper and the half-empty glass of lemonade. She opened the french doors, and went out into the garden.

After walking all the way around the house, and peering into the garden shed, she returned to the drawing room. The newspaper and lemonade remained as they had been before. Slightly surprised, but still not concerned, she went upstairs, thinking that Frank might be lying down with a headache. Finding no sign of him in the bedroom, she went downstairs again. Ignoring the dining room and breakfast room, she opened the study door. Seeing her husband lying obviously dead, with blood all around him, Miriam immediately let out a shrill scream, and backed out of the room again. After leaning against the wall for a few seconds, she moved a few yards further along the hall and sank down on the padded stool situated beside the telephone. With shaking hands she picked up the handset, and through sobs asked the operator to get the police and ambulance.

Miriam sat on the stool for several minutes, crying copiously. Then she picked up the handset again, and gave the operator another number. It took a little time to make the connection, but soon she was speaking to her daughter-in-law, Naomi Gould, living the other side of the town.

Miriam blurted out her terrible news. She had to repeat the salient points more than once, partly because her speech was so disjointed, and partly because Naomi couldn't quite believe that she had heard aright.

When that was sorted out, Naomi undertook to contact her husband at his office, and said that as soon as she had done that she would call for a taxi and come to join her mother-in-law immediately.

For the next twenty-five minutes, Miriam stayed where she was, great sobs wracking her body from time to time.

Her daughter-in law arrived by taxi only seconds ahead of her husband Martin, who had his car at the office and anyway had less distance to travel. He turned his car onto the driveway, and joined his wife as she ran up to the front door. Martin was pulling out his key when a police car pulled up in the road outside. Two uniformed officers got out and reached the front door just as Martin opened it. There was a quick exchange of names. Miriam, on hearing the voices outside, had stood up and moved towards the door.

Before her son and daughter-in-law could get close enough to hug her, she looked at the policemen and said "study", indicating the door with her finger. Martin said "we'll be in the drawing room, Inspector," as he and Naomi started to lead his mother along the hall.

"See if there's any brandy in the cabinet, darling, and pour her a stiff one. Whisky if there's no brandy.

"Can you tell us what's happened?" he asked, still with his arm around his mother.

"Your father is lying dead on the floor of the study. There's a lot of blood. There's no doubt he's been shot."

She started to sob again, before accepting the glass from Naomi and swallowing half of the double measure in one go, which caused her to splutter.

There was little conversation during the next seven or eight minutes, neither Martin nor Naomi knowing quite what to say. Then there was a tap at the door, and Martin stood to admit the policemen.

"We're very sorry indeed for your loss, ma'am," the senior man began, "but you'll appreciate that we have to ask some questions."

Miriam nodded. "I understand," she replied. "Do sit down. Martin, please move that newspaper."

"Thank you ma'am. I am Inspector Walmsley, and my colleague is Sergeant Ames. Can you please tell us what happened today?"

Miriam recounted how her husband had been in the garden when she left to go shopping, and how he must have re-entered the house at some point. She explained about the absent servants.

"He came in to get himself a drink – that lemonade beside you, Sergeant, and was reading the paper that my son has just moved. It must have been before lunch, because he knew he had to fend for himself, and there's no sign that he prepared any food.

"It's obvious what must have happened. The doorbell rang. Frank put down his paper, and went to see who it was. He took the visitor into the study – or perhaps was forced at gunpoint. Then he was shot."

"How do you know he was shot, ma'am?"

"I was in the First Aid Nursing Yeomanry during the war, Inspector – a FANY. I was in France from 1916 onwards. I've had the misfortune to see hundreds of wounded and dead soldiers, and I can recognise a bullet wound when I see one."

"I see, ma'am," said the officer respectfully. "You are of course correct. Do you have any idea who might have done this?"

"No. None whatsoever. Frank was a banker – he retired a few months ago. We've been married for nearly thirty-five years, and in all that time he's made no enemies, as far as I'm aware."

"Difficult for you to talk about this, I understand, but there's just one other thing. There is a brass cartridge case on the floor of the study, obviously ejected from an automatic pistol. I'm just wondering if the murderer brought the weapon with him, or if, perhaps, your husband brought out a gun of his own to defend himself, and got shot in a struggle."

"Yes, I understand. Well, Frank does have a pistol, left over from the war. It can't be what you're looking for, though – it isn't an automatic. Anyway, it's never been kept in the study – it's always been at the back of a drawer in our bedroom, along with Frank's socks. Wrapped in oilcloth, with an outer wrapper of cotton or linen or something. There's a box of ammunition in there too. I'm pretty sure it hasn't been used since the war."

"Gosh, Mum, I had no idea Dad kept a pistol – I've never seen it," said Martin. "I'll fetch it if you want to check, Inspector."

"Yes please, Mr Gould; but just show my Sergeant the way, if you please, and don't touch the thing yourself.

"Bring it down as it is, Ames."

"Can we offer you a cup of tea, Inspector?" enquired Miriam, who seemed to be recovering some of her usual poise.

"No, thank you, ma'am. The ambulance should be here very shortly, and then we'll all leave."

"You mean the ambulance will take the body away?" asked Naomi.

"Yes; there will have to be a post mortem examination, I'm afraid. And the Coroner will get involved."

Martin returned, followed by Sergeant Ames bearing a small parcel.

"May we make use of that newspaper to protect your little table while we take a look, ma'am?" asked Walmsley.

"Certainly."

The Inspector spread the paper out and Ames put the package down on it. At a nod from his superior, he started to peel back the cloth gently. Underneath, as Miriam had indicated, was what was evidently a pistol, wrapped in what looked like oilcloth, but which had dried out. Peeling back this layer, the gun was exposed.

"As I said, Inspector, not an automatic. This is a Webley Mark VI service revolver – it doesn't eject spent cartridges after each shot."

"I see, ma'am, yes. And it's pretty clear that it hasn't been unwrapped in a very long time. Is there a licence for it, or is this a 'spoil of war', as the saying is?"

"Oh he had a proper licence. When the new law came in – 1920 – I think – he applied for a certificate, which your then Chief Constable granted. It's been renewed every three years ever since. A year or so ago, I remember Frank telling me that under some new legislation he probably wouldn't be eligible if he was applying for a certificate now, but nobody has ever asked any questions, and the renewal seems to have been automatic.

"I'd like you to take it away now, and dispose of it."

Walmsley nodded.

"Very well, ma'am, we'll do that. I think I can hear the ambulance. May I suggest you remain here for a little while? I won't disturb you any more now, but it may be that there will be more questions in a day or so. The Coroner's Officer will keep you informed about the inquest. Good evening, everyone. Bring the revolver, Ames."

The two policemen left the room, and went to supervise the removal of the body. Ten minutes later, the three family members were left alone.

Naomi and her husband went to the study, realising that there would be blood to be cleaned off the floor before Miriam could be allowed to venture into that room again. It wasn't as bad as they had feared – it seemed that some effort had been made, presumably by the ambulance men, to clear up. Within ten minutes the room was again presentable.

CHAPTER 7

Walmsley and Ames arrived back at their police station, to find the two ranking officers – the Chief Constable and the Superintendent – waiting for them in the foyer.

"Come up to my office, all of you," ordered the Chief.

"Right," he said, before his backside had even reached the chair seat, "what have you got?"

Walmsley gave a brief summary of what they had found.

"No ideas about the killer?"

"Not as yet, sir."

"We don't have murders in this town. I'm not sure when the last one might have been, but it was certainly before my time. We don't have a detective department here, so we have neither the expertise nor indeed the manpower. We can't spare you two to investigate – and, with all due respect, you have no experience in this sort of work anyway. I'm going to talk to the Lancashire Chief Constable, and see if he can help out."

He picked up his telephone, and instructed

the operator downstairs to find the number for the Lancashire Constabulary in Preston, and ask if Mr Hordern would take his urgent call.

While waiting for telephone to ring, he looked at the Inspector again. "If the County agrees to take this on, Walmsley, I don't think their CID chaps will be happy that you have removed the body without even getting a doctor to examine it on site."

"I didn't think to do that, sir," stammered the Inspector. "I'm going to organise an autopsy as soon as possible, and inform the Coroner too."

The Chief grunted, still unhappy that criticism of his force seemed probable. The telephone rang, and he snatched it up.

"Hello Archie, David Bell here...A few months, yes... Yes...Well, we drift along usually, but today we have a problem."

The Chief explained about the shooting, and finished by asking if the County would agree to take over the case.

"What?...Really?... Oh my God!...Yes, I quite agree...Good...I'll leave that with you then... Thanks...Goodbye."

He replaced the receiver very slowly, and looked at the three officers in front of him.

"On Sunday evening, the County had a murder on their patch, involving a shooting with a pistol. Yesterday, Ashton under Lyne had a similar incident, which apparently occurred on Wednesday evening. An hour ago, Ashton asked

Mr Hordern to help them. But now we have a third very similar case, he feels that we need to call in Scotland Yard – and obviously I concur. He's going to talk to the CC at Ashton, and get his agreement before calling London.

"Get on with organising the *post mortem*, Walmsley, and tell the Coroner what's happening."

***

A few minutes past seven o'clock, Mr Hordern managed to contact the Assistant Commissioner (Crime) of the Metropolitan Police, who after hearing about the three murders immediately agreed to involve the Yard. A short discussion followed. After the call was ended, the AC telephoned a member of his team still on duty.

"Is Chief Inspector Adair still on holiday, Grantby?" he enquired. "I seem to remember he told me he was taking his wife and daughter to Blackpool."

"That's right, sir, the man replied. He's back at work on Monday, but I believe the family travels back tomorrow."

"Can you find out where he is staying, and if possible get a telephone number?"

"It may be that his Secretary has a note about it, sir – I'll take a look on her desk, and call you back."

Grantby was back on the telephone within five minutes, and informed his boss that Adair was staying in a small private hotel. He supplied the number.

Five minutes after that, the AC was connected with the Western Horizon Hotel, asking to speak to David Adair.

In the hotel, Adair and his family had just finished their evening meal, and were about to go to their room to put Sophia to bed. Muttering an apology to Becky, Adair followed the maid to the telephone, which was on the reception desk. He had a mental bet with himself as to who the caller would be, and he won.

"Lancashire has a serious problem," the AC informed Adair. "I don't think the news has reached the papers yet, so you probably haven't heard about it. Three murders by shooting, in different places and on different days, but probably connected. I've had the Lancs Chief Constable on the blower, and he's asked for the Yard's help. Sorry about this, but you are the only senior officer available – you can take Inspector Davison with you. I appreciate you're on the spot already, but I envisage that you'll want to return to London first – to take your family home and to collect work clothing and so on.

"So what I've agreed to is this. We've seen from your Secretary's notes that you're returning on the 12:05 express from Manchester. That gets in at 3:50. Take a taxi from Euston to your home. Hold the taxi, and when you've got what you need go back to Euston. Davison will meet you at the station. Take the 6 pm to Manchester

– it's another fast train which gets in at 9:15. As I appreciate you're being inconvenienced, I've authorised Davison to buy first-class tickets for both of you.

"At Manchester London Road, there's no need to take another train. A Lancashire officer will meet you, and drive you to the hotel which has been arranged for you in Preston. He'll brief you on the way. They are providing an office, plus two cars for you – and there will be a driver available for you if navigation is tricky. Have you got all that?"

"Yes sir," replied Adair resignedly. Although he had been on holiday for a week he hadn't found it particularly relaxing, and had been looking forward to a Sunday with nothing special to do. He had agreed to holiday in Blackpool to please his daughter, but three almost full days at the Pleasure Beach wasn't his idea of how to spend time away from work. (Neither he nor his wife was enamoured of The Grand National, The Big One, and other similar rides, although they certainly appreciated the effort that had obviously gone into their design and construction. However, their daughter had been ecstatic.)

Adair returned to the bedroom to break the news to Becky that he would be working again as soon as they got back to London – and with 'away' cases one never knew the duration.

CHAPTER 8

Adair's taxi got him to Euston with twenty minutes to spare. He called at the station bookstall, and then went to look for Inspector Davison. He found the tall figure standing by the platform barrier, suitcase at his feet, and joined him. The DCI, some six inches shorter than Davison and rather more rotund, looked up at his colleague.

"Hello, Barry. Lancashire to London and back in a single day for me – I'm tired already. Have you got the tickets?"

Davison deduced from the use of his Christian name that the situation was deemed to be informal, and so omitted the usual 'sir' in his response.

"Yes. The AC spoke to me personally, and said I was to buy first-class ones. I've got open returns. Just hope when I submit my expenses he remembers his promise!"

Adair grinned. "He told me the same, so don't worry. And we can dine in some style on the train.

"Ah well, another depressing away case for

us," he continued. "Given there are apparently three separate murders, I'm surprised there's only two of us being despatched. Wasn't there even a DC available?"

"I don't know, but the AC said Lancashire had promised to attach one of their own men to help. I suppose that's cheaper for them than paying for three or four Yard officers."

The two men passed through the barrier, and walked the few yards to to the first-class section of the train. There weren't too many passengers, and the two policemen found an empty compartment. They settled down opposite one another beside the window.

Each had brought a newspaper – Adair the Evening Standard and his colleague the Evening News. In addition, each had a Penguin paperback, the genres easily identified by the colour of the covers.

The DCI's was 'fiction orange' – he had first picked up *Crewe Train* by Rose Macaulay, thinking that he would shortly be on a train going through that town (where he had never been before). However, he remembered a moment later that while trains on the west coast main line did indeed go via Crewe, his train to Manchester did not. He selected *The Poacher* by H E Bates instead.

Davison's was 'crime green', having chosen *A Man Lay Dead* by Ngaio Marsh, only just published in paperback form.

As the train pulled out, only a minute past

its appointed time, each man placed his book on the seat beside him and opened his newspaper. Fifteen minutes later, via an unspoken agreement, they swapped papers, but both were sated with the contents within a further ten minutes, and sat back, looking out of the window.

They chatted desultorily for the next half hour, mainly about the current political situation in Europe.

At ten minutes to seven, an attendant opened the compartment door and invited them to take their seats in the restaurant car if they wished to take dinner. Both men rose at once. Davison had never dined on a train, and Adair had done so only rarely.

The London, Midland and Scottish Railway was rightly proud of its restaurant car service, and the police officers enjoyed their meal. Both chose the same dishes – oxtail soup, steak-and-kidney pie, and gooseberry fool – and shared a bottle of red burgundy.

They returned to their compartment for the last forty minutes of the journey, but neither picked up his book.

As the train neared the centre of Manchester, the two detectives took their suitcases down from the luggage rack, and on arrival were ready at a door. They walked almost the length of the train towards the exit gates. London Road station had more terminus platforms than through ones, and as they drew level with their locomotive it was simmering gently just short of the buffers. They noticed the name – *City of Bradford* – and both admired the streamlined casing and elegant crimson lake finish. The great machine had been pristine before leaving Euston, but now looked grubby – hardly surprising after its long journey. Neither officer would ever know that the locomotive was only a few days old when they saw it.

As they handed over their tickets at the barrier, Adair saw two men standing some twenty feet away, evidently scanning the passengers from their train. The difference in their height was much the same as that between the Yard officers. The older man was six inches shorter than the other, and probably weighed half as much. Adair nudged his colleague, and moved towards the waiting men.

The shorter of the two stepped ahead of the other.

"Would you be Chief Inspector Adair, sir?" he enquired. "And Inspector Davison?"

Adair nodded.

"Good. I'm DI Wainwright. This is Constable Fleetwood; he's to be your driver, and the Chief has said he's to be out of uniform while he works for you."

The four men shook hands, and Wainwright made the expected enquiries about the journey, and thanked the Met officers for coming. Adair smiled to himself. In his experience of 'away' cases, the local senior officer almost always thanked the visitors for coming – as though they could have disobeyed orders! Still, that was a great deal better than the occasional situation where the local man was furious at being superseded.

Fleetwood picked up the suitcases as though they weighed nothing, and led the way out of the station. He put the luggage in the boot of an unmarked Wolseley, while Wainwright ushered the Met officers into the back. Fleetwood took the wheel, and the local DI sat beside him.

As the car moved off, Wainwright half turned so he could speak to the officers on the rear seat.

"It's about thirty-five miles, gentlemen – probably do it in an hour at this time of night.

"Now, my instructions are to give you an outline of the three cases. When you come to the station in the morning, all the available statements will be on the table in your office. Also the PM reports – the last one came in a couple of hours ago. And, for what they're worth, the bullets and cartridge cases.

"The Chief Constable has particularly asked me to give you a picture of the police set-up around here. In London, I understand the Met covers almost everything, and the only anomaly is the City of London police covering the Square Mile in the middle of your patch. If you take Lancashire as the equivalent of the Met, we have twenty-seven 'anomalies' – separate forces covering cities and boroughs within our county boundary. Fortunately, we don't get a lot of cases like this one – three apparently connected murders in three different constabularies – but we do get a lot of cases where the border between the county and a borough isn't clear. It doesn't make for efficient policing.

"And some of the local constabularies – including the two involved here – have very few officers.

Outside the major cities like Liverpool and Manchester, few CID men have any experience on murder investigations anyway. So that's the background."

"Blimey," replied Adair, "I've been on cases where there were two or three police forces in the region other than the county one, but I confess I didn't know there was any with your proliferation. Perhaps that's not the right word, though – I suppose they were all around originally and have just survived."

"It is the right word really, sir. I looked into this a year or so ago. The County force was established early – in 1839 – and most of the borough forces were formed after that date. However, it is what it is.

"There was an Act of Parliament in 1888 which allowed – indeed in some cases required – some borough forces to merge with the relevant county. None merged in Lancashire, and although around the country a number of other mergers happened over the next thirty years, again there have been none here. Our boroughs guard their rights zealously!

"The office we're giving you is in the County HQ – but it isn't a public police station. The Preston police station is operated by the Borough constabulary.

"Anyway, to specifics. I'll tell you first about the killing of Aiden Cavanagh, as that's the one I've been involved with."

Wainwright briefly described the circumstances of the first murder.

"I've interviewed the entire adult population of the village. The two boys I mentioned both heard what was almost certainly the shot. Everyone around there is familiar with the sound of a twelve-bore, and one of the boys said to his friend 'that sounds like a firework'. That doesn't help much, as we already knew the time to within half an hour or so anyway. The boys saw nobody around near the wood at all. Not especially surprising; there are several exits onto three different roads.

"I've found nobody with even a minor dislike of the man. I've interviewed the managers of his two factories, who confirm that he doesn't get involved with day-to-day matters. Anyway, neither man has dismissed anyone for any reason in the last couple of years.

"The Cavanaghs don't employ live-in servants, although they could certainly afford to.

I've spoken to the two women who come in to do cleaning and so on – both have worked there for several years and have no complaints. My Sergeant suggested that Cavanagh might have been having an affair with a married woman whose husband took offence – or that Mrs Cavanagh took offence. I've found no evidence to suggest any such thing – and I've interviewed Mrs C twice and will swear that she didn't do it. She doesn't believe her husband has ever had an affair since they married thirty or so years ago."

"What about the weapon?" enquired Davison.

"Not much to go on. The bullet is point four-five-five calibre. Because the shell case was ejected – as it was in both the other murders – the gun must have been an automatic. I saw the last year of the war, and a Colt 1911 was a very popular pistol among the officers in our unit. Webleys also produced one in the same calibre, but it looked totally different and I believe had a different mechanism. There must be hundreds of these things still held by ex-servicemen – even though people are now supposed to have licences. And there may be other pistols of the same calibre."

Wainwright turned back to the front and moved his head around a few times as his neck was getting stiff. He then twisted around again.

"I can't tell you much about the other two cases. The second man was also shot while out walking, and the third was killed in his own home. Maybe you'll find fault with the way I've been handling my case, but even I with my lack of murder experience can criticise the way the locals dealt with the other two. In the second case the man was actually brought into the morgue without anyone even noticing he had been shot. In the third case the body was removed before a doctor looked at it – and since that force doesn't have any detectives no CID men saw it either."

The DI turned to face the front again, and there was silence for a few minutes.

"Have the widows been asked if they knew the other deceased men?" enquired Davison.

"When we heard about the other two cases – that was only yesterday afternoon – I spoke to Mrs Cavanagh again. She hadn't heard of either of the others. That's not to say that her husband hadn't known them, of course.

"The second victim was a widower himself, and had no close relatives to ask. I don't know what the Ashton lot did about the widow in the third case – they were certainly told about the other two cases when they contacted the County. I shouldn't say this, but I suspect that when their Chief agreed to add in their case so all three could be sent to the Yard, they just backed out.

"Changing the subject slightly, the Chief has authorised a stay for you at the Theatre Hotel in Fishergate, and rooms have been booked. A very respectable place. You could almost walk to HQ, but Fleetwood will be there to collect you at half past eight in the morning.

"It's entirely up to you of course, sir, but I've assumed you will want to spend half an hour or so reading all the paperwork by yourselves. When you've done that I'll join you again and you can ask any questions arising. Then, if it's your wish, I can take you to the scene of the first murder – and introduce you to Mrs Cavanagh.

"After that, if you want me, I'm happy to do anything else to assist. If you don't want to use me just say – I won't take offence! However, my boss says I can't help you with on-site investigations of the other two murders – that's too politically sensitive."

"We understand," replied the DCI, thanking his lucky stars that he didn't have this sort of inter-force rivalry when working on a 'home' case. There was never any problem even on the rare occasions when there was overlap between the Met and the City. The borders between the Met and its neighbouring counties were quite clear, and once it was decided on whose patch an offence occurred, that was the end of the matter.

Feeling that there was little point in discussing the cases any further, Adair changed the subject, and for the remainder of the journey the conversation ranged between life in the police and the prospect of another war.

CHAPTER 9

The two Scotland Yard officers found the little hotel very much to their taste, and after a restful night enjoyed a traditional breakfast. After that, Fleetwood arrived on schedule to take them to police headquarters, where DI Wainwright met them in the entrance lobby.

He showed them into quite a large room, containing a table, half a dozen chairs, and a telephone. On the table were a number of manila folders, three tiny cardboard boxes, and three small glass jars.

"The Chief hopes this meeting room will suit, sir," said Wainwright to Adair. "As you see, we don't have dialling facilities – if you want coffee or tea, just pick up the telephone and ask our switchboard woman – she knows you're here and she'll arrange it for you. If you want me, she'll connect you. There's a gents at the end of the corridor."

"It's fine, Inspector. Give us half an hour, as you suggested yesterday, and then come back for a pow-wow."

The Yard men sat down, and Adair pushed the boxes and jars over to Davison. "Be taking a look at that lot, and then I'll pass each statement across as I finish it. There isn't that much."

Twenty minutes later, they had both finished reading, and Adair was peering at the brass cartridge cases with a perplexed expression on his face. Eventually, he pushed the boxes aside, and looked at his colleague as the Inspector put down his last paper.

"Initial thoughts?"

"Well sir, assuming – as I think we must – that these murders are by the same man, then I'd say that they were planned. The incidents were many miles apart. Same type of victim each time – all middle-class people. I don't think this was someone just going round shooting people at random. But as to why, God knows."

"Agreed. And if they are planned, then there was quite a degree of planning involved. The killer must have known, for example, that Cavanagh was in the habit of walking his dog through that wood."

"We haven't seen the dog, of course, sir, but from the statements Tess is clearly both intelligent and friendly – happy enough to go with people she knows. But she didn't attack the killer – what about the possibility that she knew him well?"

The DCI considered this idea. "We must bear it in mind, certainly. But as you say, she is highly intelligent. Perhaps she realised that the man is holding a gun which took out her master, and realises that she's likely to suffer the same fate – and so runs off to get help. Far-fetched perhaps, but still."

He was about to say something else when Wainwright returned.

"Take a seat, Inspector. We were just talking about whether we can draw any tentative conclusions from these statements. What do you think?"

"Not random killings, sir – I'm sure of that. Same sort of victims. A long way apart. And probably carefully planned. There's some link without doubt, but frankly I've no idea what it might be."

The Yard detectives both smiled.

"Our words almost exactly," said Adair. "But whether the link is between the killer and each of the victims as individuals, or whether the victims were connected with each other as well is yet to be seen."

The telephone rang, and Adair who happened to be nearest picked up the handset.

"Chief Inspector Adair...Yes, that's correct... I'm very sorry for your loss...No, my colleague and I have only just arrived...Yes, we've seen your statement...Can you repeat that, please?"

There was a long break while the DCI was obviously listening.

"I see...Thank you, you're absolutely right... We were coming to see you today anyway...Good –

will she be in this afternoon?...Excellent..we'll see you later...Goodbye."

Adair replaced the receiver slowly, and looked at the two DIs.

"That was Mrs Gould, gentlemen – she has some interesting information which supports the 'well-planned' theory.

"It seems that Mrs G regularly went shopping alone on Fridays, travelling by taxi. One of her maids has Fridays off, so neither she nor her mistress was in the house at the time of the killing. The other maid received a telephone call very early on Friday morning. It was – allegedly – from one of her elderly mother's neighbours in Newcastle. He reported that the the mother was seriously ill and said that Annie – that's the maid – should come at once.

"Now none of this appears in Mrs Gould's statement. Nobody thought it was relevant – but it certainly is now.

"Mrs G apparently gave Annie money for the train to Newcastle, and she left immediately after breakfast. It's a long journey, and requires at least two changes of train. She didn't return that day – but that was as expected. But yesterday, after another long journey, Annie came back late in the evening. She let herself into the house, and being very tired went straight up to bed. She didn't see her mistress, and she didn't see her colleague Mary either.

"This morning, she got up and immediately

Mary informed her about their master's murder. Annie was naturally horrified, but then said that the summons to take her to Newcastle was a hoax – there was nothing wrong with her mother at all. Realising that this may be connected to the murder, she rushed along to her mistress and told her.

"Mrs Gould also understood the relevance, and spent some time trying to talk to the local police. This being a Sunday morning, there is only a solitary constable in the station, and he seems to know nothing about the murder. He also seems incapable of knowing how to contact the uniformed inspector who had originally dealt with the case. It took her nearly two hours of pressure before eventually she learned that Scotland Yard had taken over the case – she also learned for the first time of the two previous murders. Nobody thought to keep her informed.

"Anyway, as you heard, you and I will visit her this afternoon, Davison.

"Before that, perhaps we can all go to look at the scene of the first murder and if possible speak to Mrs Cavanagh and the neighbour who found the body. You'd better travel there separately, Wainwright, as you are barred from coming to the second and third locations.

"Then Fleetwood can take us to the Gould residence, and he can wait in the car while Davison and I go inside."

"That's fine, sir," replied Wainwright. "Just

one other thing. To visit the site of the Hargreaves case you'll require a local copper to guide you. As it's Sunday, I've taken the liberty of contacting the station to give notice that you're likely to want to talk to someone – the Constable who saw the body in situ, especially. The officer I spoke to undertook to try to have him at the station by four o'clock."

"Good thinking, Inspector; well done."

CHAPTER 10

The two cars – Fleetwood following Wainwright – completed the fifteen-mile journey in a little under half an hour. The three senior men stood by the side of the roadway, and the local Inspector pointed out the houses of the victim and the surgeon who had gone to search for the body. He led the two Yard detectives along the path beside Handley's property, and into the wood.

On reaching the clearing, he pointed to the spot where the body had been found. There was now no sign to show it had ever lain there.

"There was nothing in the police surgeon's report to indicate scorching around the wound," remarked Adair, "and presumably you saw no such signs either?"

"That's right, sir. The clearing isn't that wide, as you see, so I reckoned the gunman was more than five but not more than twelve or fifteen feet away when he fired."

"Yes, that must be so. But there are two things puzzling me.
Before I expand on that, tell me about the cartridge

case found here."

"It was lying on the deceased man's chest, sir. Mr Handley and his son told me they didn't go within six feet of the body, and they hadn't touched anything."

"It's very odd. Yesterday you mentioned that officers in your regiment often used Colt or Webley automatic pistols – did you ever have occasion to handle one yourself – or to see the ammunition?"

"Can't say that I did, sir, no."

"Well, you have assumed that because the cartridge was found on the body, it must have been fired from an automatic and ejected in the usual way. From their statements, the officers at the other two scenes have assumed the same.

"I was, thankfully, too young to serve in the war. However, I do a lot of shooting – with handguns and point two-two rifles on the Met's range, and with point three-oh-threes at Bisley.

"I didn't examine the the cartridge cases this morning very carefully, but a quick glance made me think. They are rimmed – which almost certainly means they were fired from a revolver, and not an automatic – which would take semi-rimmed rounds to avoid jamming.

"Now, the other thing about automatics is that most models – including both the Colt and the equivalent Webley – eject up and to the right. An ejected cartridge lands level with, or even slightly behind a stationary gunman – it certainly doesn't land way out in front. Given the distance the gunman must have fired from, in my opinion there is no way on earth that this casing could land on the victim's chest."

Both inspectors were staring at the DCI as he spoke.

"So are you saying that the killer removed the spent cartridge from the revolver, and deliberately placed it where it was found?" asked Davison.

Adair nodded.

"But why, sir?" enquired Wainwright.

"I can't imagine. But I'm sure I'm right. And, assuming the other two murders were by the same man, I think he repeated the process for those, too.

"Now, I've never shot anyone, but if I had I don't think I'd bother to break my revolver, use fingers to extract the used cartridge, and place it carefully on my victim – I'd want to get away from the scene as soon as possible. There was some reason for doing this. We have to consider, of course, that the killer was, at least to some extent, deranged, so perhaps logic doesn't apply."

There was silence in the glade for a minute, as the three detectives contemplated this.

"The business of getting away apparently unseen by anybody," said Wainwright. "I had a wander around here the next day. There are numerous places in this wood where someone could hide, well away from the pathways. I wondered if he didn't attempt to leave the wood immediately after the murder, but just waited until dark. I didn't find any specific signs, but it's still possible."

"I think that's very likely," agreed Adair. "And I suppose if he had a bit of sustenance and a lot of patience he could even have arrived before dawn, and waited for his chance. I suppose we could arrange for a thorough search of the wood, but I don't think it's worth the effort – and it's rained since Monday.

"Let's get back, and see if Mrs Cavanagh is available. If she is, what I want you to do is just introduce us, and then go back to Preston. Pack the bullets and the cartridge cases up carefully, and get someone to take them – not send them – to the Metropolitan Police lab. If you normally use the national lab at Nottingham that would be nearer, of course. If you haven't got a spare constable, perhaps you could find a suitable civilian worker. I want the things at the lab today, and a report on them by tomorrow."

"Understood, sir," replied Wainwright as the three men made their way back to the road.

As they passed Handley's house, they saw the householder in his back garden, standing looking down at a shrub. He saw the men coming, and recognising Wainwright he moved closer to the fence.

"'Morning, John, he called. "Any progress?"

"Not as much as we'd like, Stu. I spoke to Mrs Cavanagh yesterday. I don't know if she has passed on what I told her, but there have been two more similar murders. All three cases have now been passed to Scotland Yard – these gentlemen are Chief Inspector Adair and Inspector Davison. All this will be in the newspapers tomorrow."

The surgeon whistled as Wainwright spoke. "No, Alex and I haven't spoken to Muriel since Friday – her daughter is still staying with her. Can you tell me anything of the other matters – they're not in this village, I trust?"

"No – both were miles away, but almost certainly the same gunman," replied Adair. "I don't want to say any more at present, but I'm pretty sure the basic facts will have reached the newspapers by tomorrow."

"God, what an awful state of affairs," muttered Handley. "My insignificant Sunday task is to try to resurrect this dying shrub which I planted a couple of months ago and forgot to water. You have proper work to do."

"Come on Stu – most days you're saving people's lives – you're entitled look after your garden on a Sunday!"

"I suppose so. Well, good luck. If you're going to see Muriel, she's demonstrating the sort of stiff upper lip that is traditionally expected in a male, but in my experience is at least as common in the female of the species. Bless her."

The police officers passed on, and as they walked along to the next house Wainwright explained how he knew the surgeon.

The Inspector rang Mrs Cavanagh's bell, and

a few seconds later Fiona Abbott came to the door.

"Good morning Mrs Abbott," said Wainwright. "As I told your mother yesterday, Scotland Yard has been asked to take over these matters. This is Chief Inspector Adair and Inspector Davison. Is it convenient for them to speak to your mother?"

"Yes, of course; do please come in, gentlemen."

Wainwright explained that he wouldn't stay, and Fiona escorted the Met officers into the drawing room, where she introduced them to her mother.

"Do take seats, gentlemen," instructed Mrs Cavanagh. "Can we get you some coffee or something?"

"Thank you, ma'am, no; we won't bother you for more than a few minutes."

"I'm willing to spend as many hours as necessary to help find Aiden's killer, Chief Inspector. Mr Wainwright tells me that there are now three murders, and he said that although the other two were miles from here he believes them to be linked – is that also your view?"

"Yes, ma'am. My colleague and I have only been here for a few hours, but everything we've seen so far supports that theory. What we want to do next is try to establish what link there may be between the three victims."

"Yes, of course. Well, I was given the other names – Hargreaves and Gould. I've heard those surnames, obviously, but I don't recall ever actually knowing anyone with either name. And I never heard Aiden mention them either. What were their Christian names?"

"Paul Hargreaves and Frank Gould. Hargreaves was a solicitor, and Gould a retired banker. All three victims, you see, are from what we might call the prosperous middle-class – although whether that is significant we don't yet know."

"I don't even remember Aiden mentioning a Frank or a Paul. I'm very sorry."

"The other two matters took place twenty or thirty miles away, so it isn't really surprising you don't know the names. But like your husband here, each of the other men was prominent in his town.

"Now, the weapon used may have been a service revolver. Was your husband in the war?"

"Oh yes. Aiden was in the York and Lancaster Regiment. He was a substantive captain, temporary major, when he was demobbed. He hated most of his time in the army – he was at Passchendaele and other horrible battles – and when he got out he cut most of his ties. He only attended two regimental reunions in twenty years, for example.

"Anyway, I'm glad Scotland Yard is involved. Mr Wainwright seemed very nice, but when he called me yesterday he admitted that he had no experience of murder investigations."

"Our usual thought is that we see too many

murders, ma'am," said Davison, "but we always do our best to solve each case."

"That's right," said the DCI as he rose from his chair. "We'll keep you informed of progress, ma'am. Good morning."

"Thank you for coming, gentlemen; Fiona will see you out."

Back at the car, the two detectives sank into the rear seat.

"You have the addresses, Fleetwood, and my geography isn't that good. Is the Hargreaves location nearer than the Gould one?"

"No sir; the Gould one is nearer."

"All right – good, that'll let us get to the Hargreaves police station by four. Take us to the Gould place, please. And stop if you see a nice-looking public house or even a roadside café on the way – we'll all have a bite to eat together."

Fleetwood nodded obediently, but being quite familiar with the area he had immediately mentally selected a country inn some ten miles further along the road. He duly pulled in to the Goose and Gander. The three men went inside, Adair leading the way into the saloon bar.

Five minutes later, they were sitting at a table in the back garden, each with a pint of bitter in front of him. A few minutes after they sat down, a girl arrived with three huge ploughman's lunches.

"What's life like as a constable in Lancashire?" enquired Adair.

In the fifteen months the young giant had been in the force, he had rarely been addressed by anyone above the rank of sergeant. He hurriedly swallowed his mouthful of food.

"Pretty boring a lot of the time, to tell the truth, sir. I'm on the beat mostly, and not much happens. I look forward to a bit of point duty when it's offered – although your arms get tired it's sort of nice to be able to tell drivers to stop." He blushed, belatedly realising that the enjoyment of power wasn't really what traffic control was all about. However, he needn't have worried. Both his seniors had spent some time on point duty in their earlier years – they knew what he meant, and laughed.

"This is lovely fresh bread," remarked Davison. "And the cheese – would this be Lancashire? I've heard of it but don't remember having it before."

"Aye sir; it is. This sort is called Tasty Lancashire; it's matured for much longer than the Creamy type. To be honest, though – and this isn't very loyal – I prefer Cheddar!"

Both senior officers nodded.

"I wonder how much of it reaches other counties," mused Adair. "I've never seen it in a London pub, although no doubt Harrods or Fortnum and Mason would stock it.

"Why do you think you were picked to drive us, Fleetwood," he continued, "have you worked with Mr Wainwright before?"

"No sir – never even spoken to him. My Sergeant just said you were coming without a car and needed someone to take you about. He made a joke about how as I'd like to become a detective one day it'd be good to spend some time close to a couple of top ones! I think he was being sarcastic, knowing I couldn't learn anything as a driver."

The DCI grinned, thinking the assessment was probably correct.

"I imagine the situation here is much the same as in London. You have to spend time – years usually – in uniform before getting a chance to transfer. And I'm afraid it's going to be difficult to involve you in these cases. But one day, when you apply to the CID, you'll be able to say, quite truthfully, that you helped Yard detectives in three murder investigations."

Fleetwood nodded happily. He hadn't expected even to be invited to eat with the Met officers – let alone get involved with the cases.

CHAPTER 11

At almost half past one they started off again, and ten minutes later they turned into the drive at the Gould residence. Fleetwood again stayed in the car, and the others got out.

"I hope they aren't still having their Sunday lunch," muttered Adair as he banged the ornate door knocker.

To the surprise of both officers, the door was opened almost immediately, and obviously by the mistress herself.

"She gave a very faint smile. I was just by the door when you knocked – it's all right, Mary," she said to a uniformed maid who came around the corner in a hurry. "You carry on.

"Now, gentlemen, I'm Miriam Gould, and no doubt you are the Scotland Yard detectives."

Adair introduced Davison and himself.

"Come along into the drawing room," invited Mrs Gould. "Would you like anything to eat or drink?" she asked over her shoulder as they walked along the hallway.

Adair politely declined the offer, explaining

that they had only just had a meal. Mrs Gould led them into the drawing room, where her son and daughter-in law were sitting. Neither had heard the knock on the door, and looked up in surprise as the visitors entered the room.

"This is my son Martin and his wife Naomi," said Mrs Gould, "they're staying with me for a while." She introduced the police officers, and there was more hand shaking before everyone sat down in a sort of irregular pentagon.

"A very sad matter," Adair began, "and we offer our commiserations to all of you. We won't take up much of your time. I assume you have told your son and daughter-in-law what I told you on the telephone this morning, ma'am?"

Martin Gould replied. "She did, yes – and we can still hardly believe it. My father not just a murder victim, but one of the several other victims of a serial killer." He shook his head, evidently perplexed.

"You are absolutely sure that these three deaths are linked, Chief Inspector?" asked Naomi.

"As certain as we can be, ma'am. The same type of gun, and the same circumstances of leaving a cartridge case on or by the body. Also, all three victims were – how can I put this – prominent and respected members of their communities. Finding out what they might have in common is top of our list of priorities, of course.

"In a few minutes, we need to interview your servants, ma'am. But first, I'd like to ask all of you if the names Paul Hargreaves or Aiden Cavanagh mean anything to you – did you ever hear your husband mention either of those names?"

"No – I'm quite certain about that. I married Frank in 1905, and I reckon I've met all his friends since then at one time or another. I'd remember those names if he'd ever mentioned them."

"Fair enough, ma'am. Actually both the others are about ten years younger than your husband, so perhaps it's not likely they were close. What about during the war, though – did your husband serve in the forces?"

"Oh yes. He had held a commission in the Duke of Lancaster's Own Yeomanry for years before the war, and served in France and Belgium between 1916 and 1918. He won a DSO. Frank was a full colonel when he left the army in 1919, although he never used the title."

"You wouldn't necessarily know about friends and colleagues in wartime, ma'am – I guess it's still possible that he knew these other two men. His subordinates, perhaps.

"Just one other thing, ma'am. I understand that your husband was the legal owner of a revolver. Was that left over from the war?"

"Yes, it was. I don't really know why he hung onto it – to my knowledge he never fired it after leaving the army in 1919. But when they brought in new legislation, he still chose to get a licence rather than just handing it in. But I gather that it's the wrong sort of gun anyway."

"Actually, it may be the right sort of gun after all, ma'am, although of course there's no suggestion it was involved here. I asked about the war because I was wondering if the link might go back all those years.

"Anyway, I wonder if we could talk to your people now?"

"Yes, of course. Martin, please show the officers to the study. Naomi, perhaps you would find Annie and send her along.

"My husband was shot in the study, gentlemen, and I haven't yet managed to set foot in the room since then. But we must start using it again. I'll say goodbye now, in case you don't need to speak to me again today."

Martin showed the detectives to the study.

"I arrived at the same time as the police on Friday," he informed them. "I didn't come in here, with them, but they let me look in a bit later. Father was lying over there..." he pointed. "It was just awful."

"Did you notice a brass cartridge case sir?" enquired Davison.

"Yes, a shiny little thing, on the floor beside him."

As he spoke, his wife came through the door which had been left open.

"I've brought Annie," she reported, and stood aside to let the maid, a homely woman of fifty, enter.

"This is Annie Carmichael," said Martin. "These gentlemen are detectives from London, Annie.

"You'll want to talk in private, Chief Inspector, so we'll leave you. Come along, darling."

"Take a seat, Annie," instructed Adair. "Now, in your own words, just tell us what happened on Friday."

"There's not much to tell, sir," replied the maid in a noticeable Tyneside accent. "The telephone rang at about half past seven. I was passing through the hall so I answered it. There's no rule about answering – whoever's nearest, usually, whether that's Mary or me or the Master or Mistress. The call was for me – first time that's ever happened.

"It was a man. If he gave his name I didn't catch it. He just said he was one of my mother's neighbours, and someone had asked him to call to tell me that mum was very sick, and I should get over to see her straight away. He said she'd been taken to the Wingrove Hospital. Then we were disconnected.

"I was really worried. I went to ask the Mistress what I should do, and she was wonderful. Told me I must go at once, and gave me money to easily cover the return fare, and enough to take a taxi from the station to the hospital.

"It takes three trains and hours and hours to get there, so I didn't get to the hospital 'til about four o'clock. Well, when I asked at the desk, they said they'd never heard of my mother. The lady was very kind and she saw that I was upset, so she telephoned the Royal Victoria in case there had been a muddle and mum had been taken there. But they didn't know anything either. So after a bit I went to mum's house – and there she was, as right as rain. Hadn't been ill at all. She thought it was quite funny, and that someone was just playing a practical joke, but I didn't laugh. I'd had a lot of worry, and wasted a lot of time, and the Mistress had paid good money for me to travel.

"Anyway, it was too late by then to get back here that night, so I stayed with mum and started back on Saturday. Then one of the trains broke down and we were held up for hours. I got back late in the evening. I have a back door key, so I let myself in. Mary had gone to bed, so I didn't see anyone. Then this morning Mary told me what had happened. Couldn't hardly believe it. Then I realised that I'd been got out of the way, like, and went and told the Mistress. I'm so sorry that the Master was killed partly through me."

Annie ground to a halt, and looked at the DCI.

"Nonsense, Annie – you've done nothing wrong. You aren't to blame in any way. But we need to find out who called you. How many people around here know that your mother lives in Newcastle?"

The maid thought about this for a minute.

"The Master and Mistress, for sure. I've

worked here for six years, and every year I visit my ma for a week, and they know that. And Mary knows that too. I get a letter with a Newcastle postmark every fortnight regular as clockwork, so I suppose the postman knows I have something to do with the place.

"I have two special friends – they work in other houses in the town, and we all have the same evenings off so I usually meet one or both of them every week. They both know."

"Are they men or women?" asked Davison.

"They're both women. I was widowed in 1916 – my husband was killed in France – and both my friends are in the same position. We didn't know each other at the time, but I found out that we'd each decided we'd never get close to a man and risk being hurt so bad again. We just sit quiet in a corner of a pub or a little café, and don't even talk to men."

"I'm afraid you'll have to give us the names, Annie," said Adair. "Unlikely though it is, one of them may have mentioned your mother to someone else."

The maid hesitated, before seeming to make up her mind about something.

"I don't think it was them, sir. Before I give you the names, I must tell you something else.

"Mary was seeing a man recently. Two or three times she met him, on her evenings off. But then he suddenly dropped her without a word. Very upset, she was."

"Quite right to tell us, Annie. Just one more thing. The man on the telephone on Friday morning. What did he sound like?"

The maid looked as if she hadn't considered this before, and hesitated for a moment.

"Well, he sounded quite young, sir. Under thirty, for sure. Oh, and now I think about it, he didn't have a Geordie accent – his voice was like someone from around here, or maybe Liverpool."

"Good – that's just the sort of thing we need to learn, Annie. Ask Mary to come and talk to us, please. Don't say anything else."

"Looks hopeful, sir," said Davison quietly after the maid had left.

"I'd put money on this man being the killer," agreed the DCI, "but I'd also bet that we don't manage to trace him this way."

A minute later the other maid tapped on the door, and Adair called "come in".

A black-haired girl of about twenty entered the room. She was of average height, a little on the plump side, with a face that was attractive without being conventionally pretty. She wore the same uniform as Annie. She looked scared. Adair invited her to sit, and she perched on the very edge of her chair, looking down at the table.

"Now, as you probably know we're detectives from Scotland Yard in London, here to find who killed your Master – and killed two other men as well. Tell us your name," invited the DCI.

"Mary Bacon, sir," whispered the maid.

"I think you have something to tell us, Mary. If it's what I think it is, don't worry – you didn't mean any harm."

Mary, obviously close to tears, nodded slowly.

"I met this man on my evening off, about two weeks ago. His name was Vic – Victor Ford. He said he was twenty-three, and he worked doing deliveries for a baker the other side of town. We got on very well, and I saw him again the next week. Then, it turned out that on my next day off he was free too, and we spent a few hours together – in the park, and a pub, and that. We talked a lot, and he seemed interested in what the Master and Mistress were like, and what I had to do, and who else worked here.

"That day, when it was time to part, we arranged to meet again on my next free evening. That was Wednesday, but he never turned up."

The girl began to cry.

"All right, Mary, we can see you're upset. You liked this young man, I guess?"

The maid nodded, and wiped her eyes.

"Yes, sir – but now I think he was just buttering me up to get something he wanted."

Yes, thought Adair and Davison simultaneously – and not the usual something, either.

"So when you talked about Annie, you mentioned that her mother lives in Newcastle, did you?" asked the DCI.

"Yes, I think I did, God forgive me." Mary began to cry again.

"Tell us something about Vic. I don't suppose he gave you his address?"

"No sir; and he didn't tell me the name of the baker he worked for either."

"I fear that even if he had told you those things, they would have been made-up. Never mind. What about his voice, looks, height, build, and so on?"

"He's from Liverpool, I think. Quite a deep voice. Sort of medium height – a couple of inches taller'n me. Quite slim, but not like a skeleton. I thought he was handsome. Brown hair, not very long – and he had quite a bushy beard.

"He wore glasses, which suited him, somehow. But the beard didn't really suit him at all – and even before all this I did wonder if it was a real one."

"Do you mean it was on crooked or something?" enquired Davison.

"No, no." The maid, whose tears had dried up, now blushed noticeably. "On the last day he saw me, we kissed, and it didn't feel like normal hair. But I've never been kissed by a boy with a beard before, so I'm probably wrong."

Adair and Davison once again shared the same thought. However inexperienced Mary might be with hirsute males, she was almost certainly right about this beard being false.

"All right, Mary, off you go," said Adair.

"Don't keep worrying about this. If Vic was involved with your Master's murder – and that still isn't certain – he would always have found some way to do it."

The two detectives spent a few minutes discussing what they had heard, and then rose to leave. As they did so, there was a tap on the door and Mrs Gould entered the room. She cast a quick glance around, looking particularly at the carpet, before speaking.

"I understand Mary is probably responsible for giving this murderer the information about Annie. I can't bring myself to dismiss her though – she's distraught and obviously never meant any harm."

"I'm sure that's correct, ma'am," replied Adair. "I believe she thought she had found 'Mr Right', and was so infatuated that she answered all his questions about the household without remembering the conventional loyalty and discretion expected of a servant. I'm sure she'll never transgress again.

"Anyway, we won't trouble you any further. We'll keep you informed, of course."

Mrs Gould saw them to the front door, and the men returned to the car.

"Ashton police station next, please Fleetwood," directed the DCI.

CHAPTER 12

There were few cars around on a Sunday, and Fleetwood drew up immediately outside the police station.

"Come in with us," instructed Adair, "I'm sure you're in need of the gents like I am."

They were greeted by a Constable sitting behind the front desk. Correctly deciding that these were the senior officers he'd been told to expect, he sprang to attention.

DS Adams is here, gentlemen, and PC Rose is expected in about ten minutes. I'll show you the way, unless you'd like a toilet break first?"

"I think we'd like that," replied Adair, and the visitors were directed a few yards along a corridor.

Five minutes later they all returned to the foyer, and the Constable stood again and came out from behind his desk.

"Stay around here, Fleetwood," instructed Adair, "we'll not be too long."

The Yard men were led upstairs, and their escort knocked on a door marked 'CID'. There was a shout of "come in".

A burly man of forty-odd in jacket and tie stood up as the two Yard officers entered.

"I'm DS Adams, gentlemen."

Adair introduced himself and Davison, and the three shook hands.

"Please take seats, gentlemen," said Adams, "there's not much room, I'm afraid."

This was very true. Apart from the two desks, there were only two other chairs, and very little space to manoeuvre them in.

"If I may start, gentlemen," Adams began. "I understand you have two other murders apart from ours, but I have to apologise for the shambles here. On Saturday, after it was decided to call in the Yard, the Chief Constable assumed that you would arrive on Monday. He intended to welcome you and apologise in person, but we can't get hold of him today."

"All right, Sergeant. I assume you are talking about the failure to realise Hargreaves had been shot, the failure to have the body medically examined *in situ*, and the failure of the first policeman at the scene to recognise that a handgun cartridge might just be important. Your apology on behalf of your Chief is noted and accepted. None of what happened is your fault anyway. Let's forget it, and move on.

"What have you done since the body was identified?"

"I sent my DC to the crime scene, sir, but

there was no further evidence to be found there. We made house-to-house enquiries in the area yesterday, and haven't found anyone who saw anything unusual on Wednesday evening. Several people in gardens of the houses about two hundred yards from the wood heard what was probably the gunshot – that was about ten to seven.

"I interviewed the young couple who had found the body at a quarter to eight. They saw nobody else walking in the wood, and basically couldn't help at all.

"As you know, the Coroner identified the body – just as well since the man had no identification on him. Probably nobody would have reported him missing until his cleaner arrived a couple of days later – and maybe not even then.

"Anyway, when we knew who the deceased was, I took the keys found in his pocket, and searched the house.

"I couldn't find any clue there to help. His papers are all neatly filed in his study. He was comfortably off, of course – partner in the firm of solicitors. No threatening letters or anything like that.

"So I went to see Mr Firbank, and with his consent went through Hargreaves' desk in the office. Nothing remotely interesting.

"I talked to Mr Firbank. They've been partners since 1920. Hargreaves lost his wife to influenza in 1919 – they had no children – and has lived alone ever since. He didn't have live-in servants, but a cleaning woman came in on Mondays and Fridays.

"He played golf, belonged to the Rotary Club, that sort of thing. The firm doesn't touch criminal work of any kind, so there's no real possibility of a disgruntled client. Hargreaves only dealt with wills, trusts, conveyancing, and so on. He didn't even do civil court work.

"There are no relatives that Mr Firbank is aware of – and he is named as Executor in the will, which I've seen. There are no individual beneficiaries. The British Legion is to get 90% of the estate, and the local hospital the remainder."

"The Legion – so he was in the services during the war?"

"Yes sir, he had a commission in the army. Mr Firbank was apparently in the Royal Navy himself, and didn't know Hargreaves then. But he said his partner rarely spoke about the war."

"Did he say which regiment or division Hargreaves was in," asked Adair. "Both our other victims had served, although not in the same outfit as each other."

"No sir. But in Hargreaves' study there's a framed badge or shield on a wall – I think it's a regimental thing, but I didn't make a note."

"It's probably nothing, Sergeant, but so far the only possible connection between the victims is that they were all officers in the army. So go back tomorrow, if you still have the keys, and telephone me at County HQ with the details on that badge."

A knock on the door interrupted Adams' reply, and he shouted "come in" instead.

A uniformed constable entered the room warily and stood to attention.

"This is Constable Rose, sir. Rose, this is Chief Inspector Adair and Inspector Davison.

"Stand easy, Constable, said the DCI. "I'm not going into what you did or didn't do – that's a matter for your local superiors. I just have one question for you.

"The brass cartridge case. Tell me exactly – exactly – where it was before you picked it up."

Rose, who had been expected to have to listen to yet another roasting, looked astonished, and it took him a few seconds before he could speak.

"It was just beside the dead man's head, sir, maybe a couple of inches away."

"I see. And the man was lying face upwards?"

"Yes, sir."

"Anything else you remember now but forgot to say in your statement?"

"No, sir."

"Very well, that's all; you may go."

Adair looked at the ceiling for a moment. "The Doctor said in his report that he believed the man would have fallen face down after a heavy bullet struck him in the back. He suggested that the body must have been turned over after death.

"So, the man falls, inevitably away from the gunman. He's probably dead before he hits the ground, and certainly the doc says he couldn't have rolled over himself. We're back to the situation with Cavanagh, Davison. The cartridge, if ejected, couldn't reach the man, let alone get as far forward as his head. No. This confirms to me that the cartridge was removed manually, and then deliberately placed where it was found. Perhaps even on the face, and then it rolled off.

"All right, Sergeant – thank you. Let me have that information when you can. And if you find anything else, you know where we are."

The Yard officers returned to the foyer, where they found Fleetwood leaning against the front desk chatting to the Constable. Two minutes later, they were in the car and on their way back to Preston.

***

"Thanks, Fleetwood," said Adair as their driver pulled up in the yard at the back of police headquarters. "You can get off home – we'll walk back to our hotel. But pick us up again at half past eight tomorrow."

"It's gone five," remarked Adair as the two detectives went up the stairs to their office, "so especially as it's Sunday I expect Wainwright has gone home."

However, there was an envelope on the table in their room, addressed to DCI Adair. Quickly tearing this open, he smiled as he read the contents.

"Wainwright has done well," he reported to Davison. "He telephoned the Nottingham lab, and when the duty officer heard it was a triple-murder case he undertook to contact one of their experts at home. Doctor Gray, a ballistics expert, called Wainright back. He agreed to come in to look at the exhibits, and asked for an e.t.a. Wainright had worked out that going by train was very messy, but the journey was about 90 miles by road and could be done in under three hours. He'd already found a driver, so he told Dr Gray that the items would be at the lab by four o'clock.

"Gray has promised to work through the evening and night if necessary, and will give us a basic report by telephone at nine o'clock tomorrow. His written report will follow."

"Great stuff, sir. Doubt if the Met lab could have done any better in terms of speed."

"No indeed – excellent service. Nothing more we can do here tonight – let's get back to the hotel and eat."

CHAPTER 13

Next morning, the Theatre Hotel served them another hearty breakfast. For the second day running the detectives declined to sample either the black pudding or the tripe, but greatly enjoyed sausages, bacon, scrambled eggs and fried bread. At twenty to nine, they were in the office ready for the day.

The pair had hardly sat down when the telephone rang – Adair picked up the handset.

"Chief Inspector Adair...Oh, good morning Sergeant... Well done... Say that again...Well, a rough translation is 'difficulties be damned'...Yes... No, all different; we're barking up the wrong tree... All right...Goodbye."

Adair replaced the handset and looked at his colleague.

"Adams went back to Hargreaves' house. The regimental badge was for the 1st King's Liverpool Regiment. He'd noted the motto – *nec aspera tennent* – and you heard my crude translation. Damned good motto, actually.

"Anyway, none of our victims served

together. A dead end."

Both men sat staring morosely at the wall. Their thoughts were interrupted by the entrance of Inspector Wainwright.

Correctly interpreted a waving motion from the DCI, Davison gave the local Inspector an outline of what they had learned from the second and third visits the day before. There was another silence.

"Apart from the fact that these men never served together, if the maid's description is correct the murderer is a very young man – he couldn't have been in the war," observed Wainwright.

"True – my theory falls to pieces. Ah well, we'll have to come up with something else. Thanks for arranging to get the things over to the forensic people – well done."

The silence that followed lasted two full minutes, and was ended when the telephone rang again.

"Chief Inspector Adair...Yes...Oh, Doctor Gray – good morning...Yes, go ahead... I understand, yes...As expected, really... What!...Hell's teeth!...No...Right...Send it to Lancashire County Police, marked for my attention, if you please...Will you hang on to the exhibits for now?...Thank you very much indeed for coming in on a Sunday to do this...Goodbye."

Adair slowly replaced the receiver and looked from one of his colleagues to the other.

"Doctor Gray conducted the usual tests," he

said at last. "The bullets are too deformed to be compared with the rifling of a pistol – if we ever find one. However, chemical analysis shows them to be 99% lead and 1% antimony – the standard composition of service bullets used in the war.

"That is confirmed by the cases. These were all manufactured in 1917 by George Kynoch in Birmingham.

"Dr Gray examined each casing under a microscope, and he says there is no indication that these were fired – and ejected – from an automatic weapon. He suggests the overwhelming probability is that the gun used in each case is a Webley Mark VI – the same model as those held by Messrs Cavanagh and Gould.

"Apparently – and Dr Gray informed me of this with a certain relish – up to the time production ceased in 1924, something like 125,000 of these revolvers were issued. He has no real idea how many might still be in private hands, but guesses it will be in the thousands."

Adair paused.

"Now for an unexpected item in the report. On each of the cartridge cases scored – by hand – into the brass, is a number. The number can just about be read with a powerful glass – it doesn't require a microscope. But Gray thinks the writing was probably done by holding each casing in a vice and working under a fixed magnifying lens. The sort of thing used by various craftsmen – diamond cutters, for example.

"Now, here's the thing. Cavanagh's casing is '1'. Hargreaves' is '2'. Gould's is '4'.

"What conclusions can we draw, gentlemen?"

The two inspectors had been staring at him in astonishment while he was talking, and now looked at each other. Davison spoke first.

"I suppose, sir, if there is some logical reason for killing these men in a sequence, and if the gunman is really being consistent, it might mean that there is another body somewhere – number three – someone killed after Hargreaves and before Gould."

"I fear so," agreed Adair.

"But even if that's right, sir, we can't assume the final tally will remain at four. Those revolvers hold six rounds," added Wainwright.

"Again, very true. And that's assuming the man doesn't have a box of revolver ammunition."

"If there is another body, the killer couldn't have travelled very far between the murder on Wednesday and the one on Friday – so still likely to be in Lancashire," remarked Davison.

The other two detectives considered this.

"Yes," said Adair. "But I'm convinced these are all connected to Lancashire anyway.

"Well, all three murders have made the national as well as the local press this morning. I've no doubt we'll have a posse of reporters outside this building very soon. So if anyone finds another shot corpse, at least they'll know who to contact."

"I was going to tell you this when I came in, sir," said Wainwright, "but I got distracted by hearing about the forensic report. There was a local reporter here soon after eight o'clock. I sent him away, and said that if he returned at half past nine, it was possible that he might be given more information. I hope that was okay, sir – we'll have to say something, and I thought you'd need time to prepare a press statement."

"Yes, that's fine. A bit more publicity might even bring forward someone who can help us. Draft a few words for me, please. The Press already seems to have the names of the victims, but we could provide a little more – occupations, locations, dates and times, similarity of method – not much more than that."

Wainwright pulled a foolscap pad towards himself, and began to write.

Adair sat staring at the blank wall again. Presently, he rose from his chair and walked to the window, where he stood looking unseeingly through the dirty panes towards an uninteresting courtyard where several police cars were parked.

Davison, familiar with his leader's behaviour while thinking, took no notice, and simply drew the pile of papers towards him, and started to look through the statements again.

Five minutes later, Wainwright completed his draft, and after noticing the DCI apparently lost in thought, looked at Davison with an interrogative lift of the eyebrows.

Davison shook his head firmly, and held up his hand in a 'stop' motion.

A minute later Adair seemed to come out of his reverie, and returned to his seat. Wainwright pushed his draft statement across the table.

The DCI crossed out one word and inserted another. "That'll do well," he announced. "Can you get that typed up straight away? I'll go down at nine-thirty and read it to any journalist who turns up. Then your desk man can have it and read it to any others who arrive later."

"Will you take questions, sir?"

"I might – I'll want to hear the question first! I'll wait until you come back before outlining what I want done next."

Wainwright left the room, and Davison resumed his perusal of the paperwork. Adair sat with his eyes closed, but his face was now clear, and he didn't seem to be concentrating like he had been a few minutes before.

The telephone rang again just as Wainwright returned. Adair picked up the receiver.

"Chief Inspector Adair...Yes, that's right... Ah, we were half expecting this...Wait – I need to make notes...All right, go ahead... Who?...Where?...I see...Was there a brass cartridge case by the body?..Right...Go on..."

Adair now listened without speaking for a good two minutes.

Then, "Yes, I've got all that...Carry on... Yes...I see...Oh...Fair enough...What does your Chief Constable say?...Very well...All right, Inspector, please carry out these two tasks for me. First, look at the cartridge case through the most powerful magnifying glass you have. I suspect you will just be able to make out something scratched into the brass – likely to be the number three, written very small...Got that?...Next job is to go back to the sister – if she is on the telephone you can use that. I want to know, as a matter of urgency, if her brother served in the army during the war – and if so what was his regiment and final rank...As soon as convenient, send the casing and the statements to me at County HQ. And the bullet, when the PM has been done. All understood?...Good; call me back with those two bits of information as soon as possible. Goodbye."

Adair replaced the telephone receiver, leaned back in his chair, and looked at his colleagues.

CHAPTER 14

"Well, gentlemen, you'll have got the gist of that. As expected, we have another murder – very probably our missing number three.

Benedict Foster-Nash, aged forty-one, was found in his car in Blackburn yesterday evening. He had been killed by a single shot from a large-calibre weapon. The man was sitting in the driver's seat, and the shot seems to have been fired from behind at very close range. They haven't carried out the PM yet, but Inspector Boyd thinks the gunman was actually in the rear seat, rested his pistol on the back of the driver's seat, and fired downwards.

"Foster-Nash died instantly. The car was parked on a track leading to a disused quarry. Chances are that in the event of a casual walker coming across the car they would have thought the man was having a nap – he was sitting more-or-less upright with his eyes closed. And that did in fact happen.

"He was a bachelor, living with his sister. He was a veterinary surgeon, and owned a practice, but both he and his sister seem to have independent means.

"On Thursday, he left the house to go to his club – a regular habit on Thursdays, which may well be significant. His sister didn't notice he hadn't returned until he didn't appear for breakfast the next morning. She then found his bed hadn't been slept in.

"She telephoned the club, knowing that it had overnight accommodation, although her brother had never stayed there before. She was told that he had left the club at about nine-thirty, and that his car was not in the club's car park.

"By six o'clock on Friday evening, she was very concerned, and contacted the police, who weren't over-interested. On Saturday she tried again, and this time it was agreed that they would put out a message for people to keep an eye open. By Sunday she was getting frantic, but in fairness to the local coppers it's hard to see what they could do. He was an adult, and her own statement said that he had no financial or other worries, and had never mentioned suicide. The club doorman claimed he had left perfectly happily, and had said 'see you next week, Norman,' as he left the building at about the same time he usually did.

"The place where he was found was very quiet, and hardly ever visited since the quarry closed, but was less than a quarter of a mile from the club – and just inside the Borough boundary.

"Yesterday evening, a couple of lads went to

the quarry. They had catapults, and were going to play around shooting at old tin cans and so on. In fact they had been there on Saturday afternoon as well, and – as I said – saw the car and just thought someone was having a snooze. But when they saw the same car in the same place the next evening, they went over to it and took a look. Must have been a bit of a shock for ten-year-olds. Anyway, they got on their bicycles and pedalled frantically to the police station to report what they'd seen.

"It wasn't until this morning that the Borough police heard about the other cases, and of course the Chief Constable immediately said they should pass their case on to us."

The two inspectors were quiet for a moment.

"From your question about the army, sir, I assume you are still thinking there is a service connection?" said Davison.

"Yes. I have a theory. It's a bit tenuous, but may be clearer if we find that the new victim was also an army officer. A major weakness is the man seen by Mary Bacon. Skill at disguising himself is all very well, but if he was old enough to have served in the war I don't believe he could have appeared to her as a virile young man. It's still just possible that the man has nothing to do with the murders, but if he is involved I have an even weaker theory to account for it.

"Sorry to be mysterious, but until we get the information from Blackburn I'm not going any further. All I'll say is that if Foster-Nash wasn't a commissioned officer in the army, my theory falls completely and we'll have to start again. God knows where!"

Both inspectors sat racking their brains. However, they didn't have to think for long, as the telephone rang once again.

This time the conversation was very short, and ended in less than a minute.

Adair was smiling grimly as he put down the telephone.

"The case does indeed bear the number '3'. And Foster-Nash was demobbed as a lieutenant in the 1st King's Liverpool – the same regiment as Hargreaves.

"My belief is that these incidents are related to a court martial held during the last war – probably one which passed a death sentence.

"Right, I need to make a call, after which I'll go and meet the Press. Then we'll discuss what else needs to be done."

He picked up the telephone, and asked the station operator to connect him with Scotland Yard. It took several minutes for the call to go through, but eventually he was able to ask for Detective Inspector Wallace. He was about to ask the Yard operator to try another officer when Wallace came on the line. Adair identified himself, and after briefly explaining the case, issued orders.

"Drop whatever you're doing. Go around to the War Office. Ask them to dig out the service records for Colonel Frank Gould, DSO, lately of the Duke of Lancaster's Own.

"I want to know if Gould served – probably as president – on a field general court-martial during the war. If so, we need the name of the man being court-martialled, the other members of the court, the name of the officer prosecuting, the name of the defending officer or prisoner's friend, and the sentence of the court.

"I anticipate that you may get obstruction – it's fair to say they'll be a bit busy with other matters right now. So I'm going to talk to the AC, and see if he or even the Commissioner can exert pressure in the highest places.

"I don't know if it's likely, but if Gould served on more than one court martial, it's the one where an officer named Aiden Cavanagh was another member of the court.

"I imagine that if we knew the name of the defendant we could find the court martial records more easily, but unfortunately that route isn't open to us. We don't even know the year. And I've read that about three thousand British soldiers were sentenced to death in the war – of whom over three hundred were actually shot. It could take weeks to go through all those records. So going for Gould's papers is our best hope.

"It may be that they aren't even kept in Whitehall – they may be in a repository somewhere else. But they must be found.

"Have you got all that? Good. I'll give you my

number here in Preston – give me a call from the War Office to keep me informed of progress – or lack of it."

After passing on the Lancashire number, Adair asked Wallace to put him back to the Yard switchboard.

"DCI Adair here, Miss Rogers – I need to speak to the AC(C) urgently if he's available."

Adair was pleasantly surprised to be put straight through. He explained that the case was now one of four murders rather than the original three, and outlined why he was sending DI Wallace to the War Office.

"If my theory is right, sir, I fear at least one further murder, and I suspect that Wallace may not get much co-operation in the current situation. I wondered if you – or even the Commissioner – could exert some pressure in high places?"

Davison and Wainwright couldn't hear the reply, but they saw Adair smile as he put down the receiver.

"The AC knows Mr Hore-Belisha slightly, but he's going to speak to the Commissioner right away. He says Sir Philip and the Secretary of State are both members of the Athenaeum, and that connection would have more influence. He agrees that this is a case where it is entirely justifiable to put pressure on from the top.

"Now, Davidson, I want you to enquire where the headquarters of the King's Liverpool outfit is. Assuming it's still in Liverpool, Fleetwood can drive you there. I want you to go and talk to the adjutant or whoever you can find.

"See what they can tell you about Hargreaves and Foster-Nash. Specifically, of course, if they were involved together in a wartime court martial."

"We have telephone directories for the whole of Lancashire downstairs," said Wainwright. "I'll go and fetch the Liverpool one – hopefully there'll be something in that. And I'll fetch the typed press release."

He stood up and pushed his chair back just as the telephone rang again. This time Davison was sitting slightly nearer, and picked it up himself.

Within a few seconds he said "hold on just one moment, sir – I'll put you on to Chief Inspector Adair."

Putting his hand over the mouthpiece, Davison whispered "What we've been wanting, sir. It's a Dr Southgate, who says he met the three victims named in the papers – when he served on a court martial during the war."

Adair took the handset and introduced himself. For the next three or four minutes he listened intently making notes, only occasionally speaking himself to say "got that" or "I understand".

"Where are you, Dr Southgate?...Oh, right... Well, I don't think we're going to need you to make a statement. What you have told us is of inestimable value, and this information will now allow us to obtain the original documentation which we're likely to need in court.

"However, far more important is your personal situation. As you realise, it looks as though someone may be killing everyone concerned with that court martial. Clearly your own life is at serious risk. I'm going to assign a team of armed officers to your case – one of them will stay with you twenty-four hours a day from now on. Please stay in the hospital, and call a taxi to take you home – don't walk the streets under any circumstances. One of the victims was shot in his own house, so even when you're there don't open the door to anyone."

After ending the call, Adair told the others to hang on while he made more calls. Ten minutes later, he put the telephone down again with a sigh.

"All right. As you heard, I've told the AC he can call Sir Philip off now. And I've fixed some protection for Dr Southgate, who is Consultant Neurologist at the London Hospital. I'll pass on what he said in a minute – it's obviously crucial – but I'd better speak to the reporters first. Come down with me, Wainwright – you can get the typed release for me although it's now out-of-date, of course, and then bring the directory up here for Davison."

In the foyer, Adair found four reporters milling around the front desk, chatting to a harassed-looking sergeant. They took no notice of the tubby little man, until Wainwright appeared and handed him a sheet of paper. A local reporter knew the Inspector, and immediately deduced that the nondescript man must be from Scotland Yard.

Adair joined the sergeant behind his desk, and faced the journalists.

"I'm Detective Chief Inspector Adair, from New Scotland Yard. I'll read you a short statement."

He read out the words he had agreed earlier. When he finished, there was a babble of questions. He held up his hand for silence.

"I'm not taking any questions for now. However, since that statement was drafted half an hour ago, we have received some additional information. First, there has been a fourth murder in what we believe to be the same series. Benedict Foster-Nash, a veterinary surgeon aged forty-one, was shot in his car in Blackburn on Thursday evening. His body wasn't found until last night, and I can't tell you any more. We have also received an even more significant bit of information – including what we now believe is the motive for all the murders.

"If you care to return here at four o'clock I hope to be able to tell you more."

Ignoring the renewed clamour, he nodded to the Desk Sergeant, turned away, and went back up the stairs.

"I've promised to talk to the reporters again at four o'clock. Right, gentlemen let me tell you what Dr Southgate says."

Adair looked down at his notes.

"In September 1917, his regiment was at a rest camp at Poperinghe – that's quite near Ypres. There were various other units there as well. He was a captain at the time, and one day he was unexpectedly summoned by his Colonel, who told him that his services were required by another unit. He went across the camp as directed. There he was introduced to two other officers, each from other regiments. As you've guessed, one was Cavanagh, a captain like himself, and the other was Gould, then a Lieutenant Colonel. They all discovered they were to sit on a field general court martial. It turned out that Gould had sat a couple of times before, but neither Southgate nor Cavanagh had any such experience.

"The defendant was a Private John Slater, from the 1st King's Liverpool. The prosecutor was Lieutenant Hargreaves, and the prisoner's friend was 2nd Lieutenant Foster-Nash – both from the defendant's own outfit.

"The charge was basically one of shamefully casting away his arms and deserting his post while under fire.

"The evidence was overwhelming. A sergeant had given the order to stand fast, but the defendant refused to comply. He dropped his rifle, turned and ran back along the trench system. He was caught by MPs a couple of days later, several miles behind the lines.

"At the court martial, the sergeant gave evidence, as did a lance-corporal and two other privates.

"Southgate says he had sympathy for Foster-Nash, who had an impossible task. The facts of the case were not in dispute, and he couldn't even mitigate on the basis of previous good conduct, as Slater's disciplinary record was very poor.

"The decision to pass a death sentence was unanimous – as it apparently had to be.

"The warrant passed up the chain in what was apparently the usual way in capital cases. Southgate saw it when it was finally returned. A brigadier had endorsed it with 'an egregious example of desertion – recommend confirmation'. A lieutenant-general had simply added 'concur' and signed. The C-in-C wrote 'no extenuating circumstances whatsoever. Sentence confirmed'.

"Slater was shot at dawn, five days after the court martial."

There was silence for a few seconds.

"So you think some relative of Slater's – perhaps his son – has found out about the case, and is picking off those who were involved?" asked Wainwright.

"I do, yes. This is another complete guess, but if it is the son then perhaps his mother told him the facts when he reached the age of twenty-one. Or perhaps even more likely, another male relative – one who possessed a service revolver – told him. He then spends quite some time – probably months – finding out who was involved in his father's death, and then learning about them and their movements.

"But whether it was like that or not, there's one thing I'll put money on. I think our man lives in Lancashire. Partly because it's around here that he could talk to various ex-soldiers who served in Lancashire regiments. And partly because the only associated officer who hasn't been shot lives a couple of hundred miles away in London. In fact, our man might be finding it very difficult to track Southgate down."

CHAPTER 15

"So, what to do next? Carry on to Liverpool, Davison. Have you found anything in that directory?"

"Yes sir, looks like the right place."

"Good. But now the main thing you're after is Slater's address. And details of his widow, and children if any. Unlikely that she will still be living in the same house twenty years later, but still. I believe executed soldiers lost any entitlement to a pension. A tad unfair on the widows.

"But Slater's address back then would give us a starting point. Ordinary tedious police work should be able to produce an address to which the widow and perhaps her son moved, and so on down the line to today.

"When Wallace calls back, I'm now going to get him to work on the name Slater. So he'll be looking for the same as you – hopefully one of you will find it.

"Wainwright, our job will be to compile lists of Slaters in Lancashire. It's not just the Liverpool one we need now. Get someone to bring every directory you have up here, please.

"But those very probably won't help much, if at all. Your job will be to contact every single police station in the county, and ask someone to go through the electoral roll for that patch, looking for Slaters. I know it could take a week, but it's got to be done. If you have a DC or DS you can divert onto the task, that would speed up the process – just ensure that every station is covered. Better to duplicate rather than miss some.

"Any comments?"

"No? All right. Oh, just one other thing, Wainwright. If we get anywhere near to arresting this man we'll need armed officers. I'm authorised by the Met to carry a sidearm. Presumably you have some pistols here and people trained to use them?"

"Oh yes, sir. I'll get Inspector Pollard up here to discuss that with you. I know he has quite an armoury!"

"OK – off you go, Davison. Find Fleetwood for him please, Wainwright."

Both inspectors left the room, and Adair sat back, wondering just how many Slaters there might be in the county. Fifty? A hundred? A thousand? He really had no idea.

He was still musing on the 'needles in a haystack' metaphor, when Wainwright returned bearing a pile of telephone directories. He was followed by a constable carrying some more, and by yet another carrying a tray with a coffee jug and two mugs.

"Good thinking," remarked the DCI after the constables had gone, as he 'dunked' a biscuit in his mug.

"Another problem has just occurred to me," he remarked as he eyed the pile of directories. "Even if the theory about this being Slater's son is correct, suppose the widow remarried while the boy was only two or three years old? It's quite possible that he'd have taken the stepfather's surname."

"Good point sir," said Wainwright, following the DCI's example, and dunking a biscuit. "Could be we're stymied – but in the absence of any other name I suppose we have to keep searching the Slaters."

Adair nodded. "Yes; let's hope that either the War Office or Liverpool can at least give us the name of the wife – hopefully we can work from there. But actually, my theory is shaky on other grounds too. Slater may not have been married, and whether he was or not he may not have had a son."

"Dickens of a job to trace even a son with the name Slater, sir – anything else is going to be a nightmare."

"I must admit I'm not confident. And I suppose I should depress you even more by pointing out that the boy – if he exists – might be little more than twenty-one. It's possible that he wouldn't yet have appeared on the electoral roll."

"Oh, God," muttered the DI, shaking his head sadly.

"All right, sir; I've split up the various areas between my DS, a DC and me, so I'll make a start."

He just reaching for the telephone, but Adair stopped him.

"Hang on for a few minutes – look at some telephone directories first while I make a few calls to update people."

Over the next twenty-five minutes Adair spoke to two chief constables and to Inspector Boyd. He then called Mrs Gould, Mrs Cavanagh, and Miss Foster-Nash in turn. He was unable to get hold of Mr Firbank, but left a message for him.

Letting out a long sigh, he pushed the telephone towards Wainwright.

"Do you know if your Chief is in the building? I need to talk to him too."

"Don't know, sir, but I can call his secretary for you."

"No, I could do with stretching my legs. Where's his office?"

"Top floor, sir; right at the end. You come to the Secretary's office first – that's Mrs Leadbeater."

"Right. When I get back I'll take over the directory job, and you make a start with the electoral rolls."

"Okay, sir, I've been through two of them, and found about twelve Slaters. I've started a list, here. The directories I've done are on the floor."

Adair opened the door just as a uniformed

officer with a lot of silver on his epaulettes was about to enter the room. Wainwright jumped to attention.

The officer held his hand out to Adair. "I'm Archibald Hordern," he announced; "thanks for coming all this way to help. Do sit, both of you. What's the latest?"

"I've just been updating the other chief constables involved, sir, and I was just coming to see if you were in."

The DCI gave the Chief Constable an outline of the situation. Hordern shook his head sadly.

"A fourth murder – what is the world coming to? So you're confident about the connection between the four, but not too sanguine about identifying the actual gunman?"

"That's correct, sir. A lot of unknowns as yet. We should hear from the officers looking into army records in London and Liverpool sometime this afternoon.

"However, I'm contemplating making use of the newspapers and wireless. The reporters are coming back at four o'clock hoping for more information. I could outline the 1917 court martial thing, and ask them to put something in their papers about the police wanting information about the relatives and friends of the man concerned.

"That's highly risky, of course. Ideally, we wait until – hopefully – we have a name. Then we can legitimately issue a statement saying that we are interested in interviewing the man – without mentioning the case at all.

"But in either instance the culprit might panic. He could flee. Or he might do something stupid, and shoot some innocent person who approached him. Tricky."

Hordern nodded slowly.

"Well, you decide what's best. You've done very well to get as far as you have in such a short time. One thing, though. When you get near to this man you need to be armed or at least have armed officers with you."

"That's in hand, sir," interposed Wainwright. "Inspector Pollard is coming up shortly to discuss it."

"Good; well done. Keep me informed of developments."

The Chief Constable left the room, and Adair and Wainwright restarted their searching.

Forty minutes later, as Wainwright was replacing the telephone handset after making his sixth call, and Adair was throwing yet another directory onto the floor, their eyes met.

"Do you have a canteen or something in this building?" enquired the DCI.

"Well yes, but it's pretty basic. Sandwiches, made to order usually – cheese, egg, ham. Soup. Toast with scrambled egg or beans or cheese. One hot meal which is usually sausages and mash, or sausages and chips. We get a fish dish on Fridays.

"Or there are several cafés within walking

distance."

"Oh no – the sausages sound very appealing. I'm happy with them. Let's do another fifteen minutes here, and then if you're hungry too we'll go."

However, within two minutes there was a tap on the door, and another uniformed officer arrived. This one was much younger than the Chief Constable, and also taller and thinner. Wainwright smiled a greeting.

"Sir, this is Inspector Pollard; Keith, this is Chief Inspector Adair."

Take a seat, Inspector," instructed the DCI after shaking hands. "You've heard about the situation, of course."

"Yes, sir. I understand that you will carry a gun yourself, and within reason I can supply you with as many armed men as you might need – obviously it'll depend on the circumstances. I'll come myself.

"We have various sidearms you can choose from – what do you prefer?

"A Colt M1911A1, but I can use almost anything else. A revolver if you don't have an automatic."

"Bless you sir, we have several M1911s. I'll fix you up with one of those, plus a couple of clips and a box of point four-five ACP ammo in case you get involved in a shooting match.

"Should you need anything longer range, we have a few three-oh-three SMLEs, and a sergeant who can take one and hit the bull at five hundred yards on the local army range. Or I can provide a nice pump-action Winchester 12 if you need a shotgun," he added enthusiastically.

Adair laughed. "Well, as you say, it'll depend on the circumstances. But it's likely that me with the Colt plus you and perhaps one other officer also with handguns should be enough."

"Fair enough, sir. Pity, really. Since I've been in post I haven't had to issue firearms for any situation within our patch. In the last eighteen months we've helped out Liverpool three times and Manchester twice, but otherwise the only time I unlock the store is when one or more of the six trained officers go to practise on one of the ranges.

"Do you want the Colt now, sir? You'll have to sign the book, of course."

"Not yet, thanks. I'll wait until we find someone who might be carrying. But hopefully that won't be too far ahead."

After Pollard had gone, Adair stood up again.

"Let's go and eat."

***

Half an hour later, having partaken of the promised sausages with mash and peas, a vanilla ice cream with wafers, and two cups of tea, the DCI felt like a new man. Back in the office, he and Wainwright recommenced their respective tasks.

After three more telephone calls, the

Inspector put down the telephone again and crossed another line off his list.

"If by four o'clock we don't hear anything from Mr Davison and your man in London, will you give the reporters more details and ask them to broadcast them?"

Adair closed the directory he was perusing and dropped it on the floor.

"I can't decide. It isn't just asking the public for information. As you know, a few of the papers – particularly the Sunday ones – have some pretty dogged investigative crime reporters. If I give them the facts about the court martial, they could well find out what we want. I wouldn't mind if they got there first, but I would mind if one of them got shot for his pains. I'll play it by ear.

"I've finished the directories; how are you getting on?"

"Done all those on my list, sir, so I'll go down to the CID office and see how my lads are doing."

"Good. Then we can cross-check the addresses from the directories with the addresses from the electoral registers, and also see which names only appear in one place. There must only be a tiny minority of the public on the telephone – these directories are pretty thin – and certainly there are very few Slaters listed. The list from you and your men will hopefully be much longer."

Wainwright left the room, and Adair sat staring blankly at his list. Slater B, 23 William St., Slater G, Rose Hill House, Slater K, baker, 102 High

Street – and some thirty others spread across eight towns. None, he realised, was likely to be the killer – but one or two on the list might be related to him.

The telephone rang again, and found it was Inspector Wallace, calling from the War Office.

"They're being quite helpful, sir. I've got the file on Colonel Frank Gould. Not really sure how it will assist you, though. It's very thin, and there's no mention of presiding over a court martial."

"Not to worry. We've found the name of the man who was being court martialled now – make a note of this, Wallace. It was Private John Slater, of the 1st King's Liverpool Regiment. Start digging for his details. I don't know when he joined up, but he was shot for desertion in 1917. I desperately need to know anything there is about his address at the time, the name of his wife if he had one, and the names of any children recorded.

"I think it more likely that the records of a private soldier will be held with his local unit, and Davison is looking into that now. But we must leave no stone unturned. If you can find Slater's court martial records your end, then there may be some mention of his next-of-kin. See what you can find."

The DCI resumed his blank stare.

CHAPTER 16

Twenty minutes later, the telephone rang again. This time Adair heard the excited voice of his DI.

"Got here and found the barracks easily, sir. I saw Major Yates, the Adjutant, and he's been very helpful.

"To cut a long story short, I've seen Slater's records. He married Harriet Wales in late 1915. In January 1916, when conscription came in, he as a married man was exempt, but when the law changed again in May he was called up. They were pretty desperate for men, of course. The adjutant says in normal circumstances they'd never have considered Slater – the records show that they knew he'd already served two sentences of imprisonment in civvy street.

"It's recorded that his wife gave birth to twin boys on November 23rd 1916. Their names are not shown – the only reason it's noted at all seems to be that he was granted special leave of some sort to come home for a week.

"As we know, he was executed in September 1917. After that there is only one note on his file

– that in March 1918 his widow married Company Sergeant Major Jacob Dawes – a member of the same regiment.

"They found Dawes' records for me. A far better soldier all round – joined as a volunteer in 1915. Won a Military Medal and a Distinguished Conduct Medal. He was demobilised in 1920, and his last address was 57a Highgate Street in Liverpool. There is no entry later than when he was demobbed.

"Oh, and Major Yates says that in the war warrant officers were sometimes issued with service revolvers, just like commissioned officers.

"He mentioned in passing that Lancashire didn't have an entirely unblemished record in the war. There were of course numerous acts of almost unbelievable bravery, and VCs and so on, but of the three hundred or so soldiers executed during the conflict, thirty-one came from Lancashire regiments. Our man wasn't even the only one in the 1st Liverpool outfit."

"Well done, Davison, that's all very helpful. Let me think for a minute."

Adair paused, his brain racing, just as Wainwright returned, clutching more papers.

"All right, Davison, there are two prongs to this now. I'll get someone to check in Somerset House for the boys' names.

"Then there's work to do in Liverpool. We need to follow up the Highgate Street address, and also see what trace can be found of Dawes. Since you're already there, you'll have to make a start. However, we need to let the Liverpool boys know you're working on their patch. Give me twenty minutes, and then call me back."

In a few words, the DCI passed the outline of Davison's findings to Wainwright.

"Mr Pollard said he'd worked with Liverpool officers before – have you had any contact with their CID?"

"Oh yes, sir; several times. I can contact DI Heaton, or DCI Webber, and inform them."

"Good; do that please. If you can get hold of one of them, just say that Mr Davison is on their patch, working on the quadruple murder case. This is just a courtesy call – we aren't asking for their help at this stage."

Wainwright nodded, and picked up the telephone. Within two minutes he was talking to his acquaintance, and three minutes after that he replaced the receiver.

"Right, sir; no problem. DCI Webber says we only have to ask and he'll provide some more officers."

"Excellent. Right; I've time to contact London before Davison calls back."

Picking up the handset himself, he gave the number for Scotland Yard. Making the connection took another five minutes, but eventually he was talking to one of the detective constables in his department.

"I don't care what you're doing, Wheeler,

this takes priority. Get across to Somerset House immediately. Don't walk, take a tram. Check births for me. On November 23rd 1916, twin boys were born – almost certainly in Liverpool – to a Mrs Harriet Slater. I need to know the full names of those two children. If you don't find anything on that date, check one or two days either side of it. I don't need copies of certificates or anything, just the basic information. Understand? Right; call me back here the minute you've got it."

Adair replaced the handset, and smiled at the local DI.

"We're making progress. I must say I hadn't envisaged twins when I thought we might be looking for a son. And we still don't know if the boys might have taken the stepfather's surname.

"But one thing does occur to me."

Adair looked through the pile of telephone directories still lying on the floor, and selected the one for the city of Liverpool.

"Oh joy!" he exclaimed after a few seconds, "there's a Dawes J, watch and clock repairer, at 37 Platt Street."

"Just the sort of man to have one of those bench magnifiers you talked about before, sir."

"Yes; and rather more probable than finding a diamond cutter hereabouts!"

The telephone rang, and Davison was on the line again.

"We have more information," Adair told him. "It's possible that the man Dawes runs a watch repair business at 37 Platt Street. This needs to be handled delicately.

"Fleetwood doesn't look like a policeman, and he has the advantage of sounding Lancastrian, if not Liverpudlian. Send him to this address by himself. He should just ask some harmless question – such as how much would they charge to take a look at a watch which runs slow. With a bit of luck it'll be a one-man firm, and he can see if the age of this bloke conforms to that of ex-Sergeant Major Dawes, who will be somewhere around fifty.

"He can also see if it looks like someone lives over the shop. We can't be lucky enough for him to see the wife, let alone the stepsons, but you never know. Tell Fleetwood not to say anything to raise suspicions.

"While he's doing that, you get onto the council, and see if you can find out who pays the rates on 57a Highgate Street. If it's not Dawes, see if they can show you where he might have moved next. But the shop looks to be the better bet."

"The Liverpool boys know you're in their city – they're happy. Get back to me as soon as you can. Tell Fleetwood that if he finds anything important not to wait until he meets up with you again – he should call me from a public kiosk."

He replaced the handset.

"I see you've got your lists now. What do you have in the way of Slaters in Liverpool?"

Wainwright shuffled through his papers.

"Eighteen of them, sir. But our suspects will

be twenty-two years old now, and none of these are under thirty."

Adair grunted. "There are three Slaters in the Liverpool telephone directory – no doubt they're among those on your list, but we'd better just cross-check."

It was the work of a few seconds to show that the three Slaters on the telephone were indeed among those on the electoral roll.

"All right; it won't take my DC many minutes to get to Somerset House, but I've no idea how long a search takes. I think we have time for a cup of tea while we wait – there nothing more we can do for now. Although I suppose we shouldn't abandon the telephone – can you have something brought to us again?"

The DI nodded, and gave an order via the telephone. Within five minutes, two cups of tea and two slices of rather dry Madeira cake were delivered. The two officers sat in companionable silence for the next ten minutes.

Adair had just started to speak when the telephone rang again. He picked up the handset.

"Yes, Wallace...I see...Can't be helped... No, we've gleaned some useful stuff from the barracks up here...No, you can abandon this now... Thank the people who've been trying to assist... Yes...'Bye."

"No further information from the War Office," reported Adair. "I'm just going to the gents."

On his return, the DI informed him that the front desk had reported the arrival of several reporters. Adair grimaced.

"Decision time. But they're a bit early – I'll keep 'em waiting a bit longer."

He sat, quite still apart from drumming his fingertips on the arm of the chair. Another few minutes passed, and the telephone rang yet again.

"Chief Inspector Adair...Hello...Really?"

The DCI now listened in silence for nearly two minutes without interrupting.

"That's great...Very well done, Constable... Have you arranged to meet up with Mr Davison?...Good, do that...No...When the two of you get together, ask him to call me here, and by that time I may have a plan...Thanks – and well done again."

He put the telephone down again, and turned to Wainwright, smiling happily.

"Fleetwood has come up trumps. The shop is quite close to the barracks, and he found it quickly. There is a sign on the door saying 'Closed owing to death of the Proprietor'.

"So your Constable used his gumption, and went into the adjacent shop – it's a newsagent/tobacconist sort of place. Fleetwood told the woman behind the counter that he left a clock next door months ago, for repair, but hasn't been back to collect it as he's been overseas – made out he was a sailor. There were no customers in the shop, and the two of them had a good gossipy chat. He learned several facts.

"First, Dawes died about two months ago. Second, the 'J' does indeed stand for Jacob. Third, his wife – and it was Harriet – died a year or so before him. Fourth, the two of them did live above the shop – but only for the last five years or so.

"Perhaps most important, Harriet told this neighbour when they moved in over the shop that it was because their two boys had now left home. So that all ties in.

"Now the neighbour can't remember Harriet ever mentioning the names of the sons. She can't remember them coming to the shop as children either. But the old duck does remember that Harriet told her that Jacob was only the stepfather – she actually said 'that's why their surname is different'.

"But she said she'd seen one young man come several times since Jacob died, and use a key to get in. The last time she saw him was about a week ago, but she admitted that she wouldn't necessarily see every visit.

"She suggested that Fleetwood should put a note through the letter box providing his address, and ask how he could reclaim his clock. Fleetwood agreed – with a straight face, he tells me – that he would do that.

"We're getting nearer, Wainwright. I'm going down to see these journalist fellows; I don't think I'm going to give any more detail after all, hoping that we get the names ourselves soon."

"Do you want me to come in support, sir?"

"No point in having them hate you as well as me! Stay here in case Davison or Wheeler call."

The DCI was back within ten minutes.

"Well, they're grumbling, of course. They rightly suspect that we have information that we aren't passing on, and a couple of men from national papers kept pressing me. I gave a bit more detail about each of the four murders, but limited it to that.

"Has anyone called?"

The DI was just shaking his head when the telephone did ring.

"Adair...Hello Wheeler...Good...Okay, I've got that...No, nothing more, get back to the Yard... Thanks, and well done."

Once more Adair turned to his colleague, this time with a smile even more radiant than the one before.

"Stephen John Slater and David John Slater. I wonder. Get on the phone to your Liverpool colleague again. Give him those names and enquire whether either of them has a criminal record – if so that'll be the easiest way to get an address."

He pushed the instrument over to Wainwright. After getting through, the DI spoke for a few seconds, and then hung up again.

"DCI Webber says the name Stephen Slater sort of rings a bell, but he's going to talk to someone in the uniformed branch and call back."

Before the senior Liverpool officer could ring again, DI Davison called. He had joined up with PC Fleetwood, and had heard about his findings at the shop. His own research had not been productive, as Dawes hadn't been involved with the Highgate Street address since 1922. He asked for instructions.

"I haven't decided how to handle this yet. There's the result of one more enquiry to come. Where are you now?"

"I see. Just wait there, and then call me back in fifteen minutes."

He had hardly put the telephone down when the Liverpool officer called back. Adair introduce himself.

"I've spoken to my colleagues," Webber reported. "There's no record for David Slater, but Stephen Slater has several previous convictions. He was charged with assault twice when only fourteen, and was birched on the second occasion. After a case of theft when he was fifteen he was sent to an approved school, and stayed there for a year. At seventeen he was again convicted of assault, and sent for two year's Borstal training. Earlier this year, now an adult, the magistrates gave him three months for criminal damage – he defaced a war memorial. And the bit you probably want is the last known address – 113 Bantock Street. That's a back-to-back style terraced property – only one way in and out."

"All very useful; many thanks," said Adair.

"As you know, I have a Yard DI in your city, with a county Constable. Can I send them round to your station to wait while I decide what to do next?"

"Of course, we'll make them welcome. I'm at Westminster Road."

Davison called back a few minutes later.

"Go to Westminster Road police station. See DCI Webber – he's expecting the pair of you.

"I doubt if there is a court in session now, so ask him for details of a local magistrate. Write out an 'information', outlining the situation regarding the four murders. Go and swear that before the JP. Request search warrants for 113 Bantock Street (Mr Webber will explain where that address comes from), and also for the shop and the living accommodation above it. Hopefully they'll be granted.

"I'll come to Liverpool myself shortly with a couple of armed officers. I'll meet you at the police station. Hang on a second."

Adair turned to Wainwright. "How long will it take us to get to Liverpool?"

"A bit under an hour, probably."

"All right, Davison, we'll see you in about an hour."

The DCI put down the receiver.

"If Inspector Pollard is still here, please ask him to find me a pistol now. I also want him to arm himself, and come up here as soon as possible. I think two of us being armed is sufficient."

Ten minutes later, Inspector Pollard arrived,

carrying a cardboard box and a book.

"Will you just sign the register, please sir?" he said to Adair.

That done, he slid the box over to the DCI. He then delved in his pocket and produced a much smaller box which he also pushed across the table.

Adair removed the lid from the larger box, and withdrew a holstered automatic pistol and a spare ammunition clip. He took the pistol from its holster, and removed the empty clip already in it. Then, breaking the seal on the smaller box, he shook out some bullets and proceeded to load both clips. He snapped one magazine into the butt of the pistol, and dropped the other in his jacket pocket.

"I see you have done that a good few times before," remarked Inspector Pollard, who had been looking on approvingly.

"Yes," replied Adair, "but so far I've only shot on the range. I've had to draw a gun a couple of times on duty, but so far I've never had to fire."

"Likewise," said Pollard. "I hear it's different in America, though."

"Ah yes; but here we don't allow every Tom, Dick and Harry to have even one firearm without a licence – let alone as many guns as they want!

"What are you carrying yourself?"

"I have a Colt Super point three-eight, sir."

"Good. Now, it's only fair that you come, Wainwright – and in fact you can drive us to Liverpool in your car. Davidson and Fleetwood have theirs, so the three of us can all go in the same one.

"But you'll have to take a back seat during the actual arrest – if we get that far. Let's go."

CHAPTER 17

The journey to Liverpool was uneventful. The DCI sat in the back with Inspector Pollard. Although their route passed through countryside for the most part, there really wasn't much for Adair (who had never been to the city) to see on the journey. The three officers conversed on various topics, most connected with police work – all had interesting experiences to recount – but none relating to the case in hand.

At the Westminster Road station, Wainwright parked next to the car he recognised as Fleetwood's, and the three officers went inside. A cheerful Desk Sergeant immediately identified them and bade them welcome.

"Mr Webber and your chaps are having a cuppa in the mess room, gentlemen – just go down to the bottom of that corridor."

In the little mess room, introductions were made. DCI Webber proved to be a huge bear of a man, larger even than Fleetwood. As the senior officer called to a woman by the tea urn for three more cups, Adair couldn't help thinking that in a rough house he would be a good man to have beside you.

When everyone was settled again, Davison passed two documents to his boss.

"No problem with the warrants, sir," he reported. "The JP said he hoped we get our man very soon – he reckoned four murders is really damaging the county's name."

"Before you discuss how you're going to play this, I'll disappear," said Webber. "I'm approved for carrying firearms and I'd love to come on your raids, but your team is already top heavy – a DCI and three Inspectors to no sergeants and one constable!"

Adair grinned. "Certainly unusual," he agreed. Anyway, many thanks for your help. It'll go in my report, of course."

When Webber had gone, Adair looked around the room. Nobody else was now present – even the tea lady had gone.

"Right. We'll go to the Bantock Street address first. I see you have a street map there, Fleetwood. Let Mr Pollard take a look now so he knows where Bantock Street is, in case the cars get separated on the way.

"Now, I'm told that this is a back-to-back property – the front door is the only way in and out. Mr Pollard and I will go to the door – the rest of you stay in the cars until I say otherwise. Keep your hand on your pistol, Pollard, and be ready to draw it, but I don't think we need to brandish guns in the street.

"I'll decide what to do about the shop depending on what we find at Bantock Street. Questions?"

There being no questions, everyone trooped out to the cars. The journey took barely five minutes, and the cars turned into Bantock Street together. The area was one which might be termed poor but respectable – every small property externally identical, but most seemed to be painted and otherwise well cared for. Fleetwood drove along slowly looking for number 113. Just ahead of the car, walking in the same direction, was a woman carrying a shopping basket, and the driver pulled up almost beside her as she stopped – clearly by the house they wanted.

As agreed, Adair jumped out, and Pollard was with him in a couple of seconds.

The woman – she was little more than a girl – had put her basket down on the step and was about to put her key in the door. She turned in surprise. Seeing the uniformed policeman, she seemed to sway, and leant against the door.

"Has something happened to Dave?" she asked breathlessly.

"No, no, nothing like that," replied Adair. "Will you tell us who you are?"

"I'm Alice Slater; I live here with my husband," the girl replied. "What do you want?"

"We want to speak to your husband, if he is David Slater; perhaps even more, though, we want to speak to his brother Stephen. Is he here?"

Mrs Slater stared at him.

"Stephen doesn't live here – never has done. I can well understand you wanting to speak to him, but my Dave's never done anything wrong in his life. He'll be home quite soon now. You'd best come in and wait."

"Very kind, Mrs Slater. But we'll just change my team around first."

He turned to Pollard. Just ask Messrs Davison and Wainwright to come in, and you wait in the car with Fleetwood. Keep your eye on the street," he added *sotto voce,* "and when this chap comes just meet him to see he isn't carrying a gun before he comes in."

The two DIs joined Adair, and the girl looked at them curiously as she showed them straight into the little living room.

"Please sit down," she said, "I can get you all a cup of tea if you like?"

Adair declined the offer with thanks. He and Davison took the two armchairs, while Wainwright sat on one of the three dining type chairs. Mrs Slater took another. They all looked at one another. The detectives saw a pretty dark-haired girl of perhaps twenty, neatly but certainly not expensively dressed. The DCI introduced himself and his two colleagues, at which Mrs Slater looked even more bemused.

"Three senior policemen – and the one in uniform outside – he was an inspector too, wasn't he? My God, this must be something bad!"

"Adair didn't answer the implied question, and merely said "you may be able to help. You say Stephen Slater doesn't live here? But this is the address he has given the police in the past."

"I know. He's Dave's twin, and he puts this address down sometimes if he needs somewhere for letters to reach him. He's never had what you'd call a proper address – nor a proper job for that matter. So Dave allows him to give this address, and every now and then Stephen comes to pick up any letters. He only comes when he knows Dave'll be here though – he knows I won't open the door to him. He's never ever been inside the house, not once."

"Tell us first about your husband. A twin, you say?"

"Not identical, but a twin, yes. They say Dave takes after his mother, and Stephen after his father, who was also a very bad man. Dave works on the Overhead Railway – he's a ticket office clerk at the Alexandra Dock station. He's worked for the LOR since he left school. I work at the greengrocer's round the corner – we do all right."

"Thank you. Now, we understand that Dave's mother died a year or two ago, and his stepfather quite recently?"

"That's right. I knew Dave at school, and I met his mum a good few times over the years before we married – lovely woman she was. She lost her husband in the war, but married Jacob

Dawes soon after. A good man – she was lucky to get him after the first one. He was like a real father to the boys too, although Stephen has repaid him badly. When the brothers left home, Harriet and Jacob moved to live over Jacob's shop – he sold and mended clocks and watches and things."

"Do you know how their father died in the war?" asked the DCI.

"Yes," said Mrs Slater, reddening slightly. "But none of us knew until after Harriet died. The boys knew Jacob wasn't their father, of course – they didn't have his name. But their mum would never talk about it. When Jacob knew he was dying himself – about six months ago, I suppose it was – he told them what had happened to their real father.

"I wasn't there, but Dave said his brother was furious, and started shouting and swearing and threatening revenge. When Dave told me about it, later that evening, he just said he was disappointed to hear about his father, but not really surprised."

The girl suddenly stopped, and looked at the detectives with a horrified expression on her face.

"People of your rank coming here," she blurted; "this isn't one of Stephen's usual offences. It's something to do with these recent murders, isn't it?"

Adair nodded. "I fear so. Do you know where Stephen is at present?"

Mrs Slater shook her head. "I'd tell you if I

knew. And I'm sure Dave would too."

"The shop, Mrs Slater. Would Stephen be living there now?"

"No sir." He has a key, like Dave has. But Dave made it very clear to his brother that he couldn't spend even one night there, making the place unfit to show people around. You see, Jacob owned the freehold, and after Harriet died the property comes to the brothers. Actually two thirds to Dave and one third to Stephen, which caused another row between them – but Stephen knows it's in his interest that the place is sold for the best possible price.

"Dave goes in to check twice a week, and he would soon see if his brother had been sleeping there."

"I honestly don't know where Stephen is. He always seems to have money, but none of it comes legally, I'm quite sure of that."

The sound of voices just outside the window came to them, and as the street door opened Mrs Slater jumped up and ran the few steps across the room to hug her husband.

David Slater, having already spoken to Inspector Pollard, was half prepared to see the other policemen. His wife couldn't remember their names, so this time Davison did the introductions.

Slater, dressed in railway uniform, perched on one of the chairs at the table, with his arm around his wife.

Before Adair could start asking questions, Alice Slater put her husband in the picture.

"They think Stephen killed those four men we read about in the paper," she burst out.

"I didn't actually say that, Mrs Slater," responded Adair. "I only said we want to talk to your brother-in-law."

"You don't need to wrap it up nicely, sir," replied Slater. "I know only too well what my brother is like. He's been in trouble, mainly for violence, since he was seven or eight years old. First at school, then with the police and the courts. But murder? And why should he kill those particular people? They were miles away from Liverpool, weren't they? Oh, and I see now why the policeman outside patted me down – he was looking for a gun, I suppose."

"Yes. Now, your wife has told us how Stephen reacted when your stepfather told you about what happened to your father."

"That's right – he was hopping mad. But so what?"

"All four murder victims were directly involved in your father's court martial."

Slater looked stunned. "I see," he muttered at last. "I haven't seen him for something like six weeks. I did wonder what he was doing – thought he'd probably been sent to prison again."

"You don't know where he's been living recently?"

"No. I have no idea. To be honest, I don't

want to know anything about him. He's my brother – I can't escape that fact. So I let him use this address as a sort of post box. But that's as far as I'll go. And that was before I knew what you've just told me," he added.

Inspector Davison took over the questioning.

"Tell us about Mr Dawes' shop. He and your late mother lived there for some years, we understand."

"That's so, yes. They moved in above the shop about six years ago. I used to visit quite often, and Alice came too after we started courting. Mum died, but we still visited – Jacob was the only father I've ever known, you see. He was always good to us – a role model, as they say – but for some reason Stephen didn't follow his example."

"When did you last look over the shop and the living quarters?"

"Yesterday; I went there on my way home from work. The agent was taking a possible buyer around this morning, and I just wanted to make sure the place was still fit to be seen."

"And was it?"

"Oh yes. If you're thinking my brother would stay there you can think again. I made it quite clear that he was not to do that – not even for a single night. And he'll obey me – I'm one of the few people he's a bit scared of, ever since I beat him up when we were both about twelve.

"But hang on, sirs. These murders were by

someone using a gun. Where would Stephen get that?"

"Well, unfortunately it's not that hard to get hold of one if you know the right criminals," said Adair. "But the revolver used is one specifically issued to soldiers during the war. Your stepfather was a warrant officer in the army and might well have been issued with one. Did you never see one in the house?"

Slater shook his head.

"But I can say this. Jacob – we were always told to call him that even as little kids – was in hospital for nearly a week before he died. I didn't go into the shop between Jacob going into hospital and his death, but I know Stephen visited him and took the keys, because he told me later that he had looked in two or three times 'to keep an eye on the place' as he put it. If Jacob had a gun, I guess Stephen could have found it and taken it then."

"All right, Mr Slater. Let me have your keys for the shop premises, please. We actually have a warrant to enter, but it'll be much better to go in with your consent.

"You're welcome to join us," he added as Slater took two keys off his ring and handed them over.

"No thanks – just bring the keys back when you've finished, please. You won't be turning the place over, will you? We may have more viewers."

"Nothing like that; don't worry. Why two keys?"

"One key is for the shop, the other is for the living area upstairs. Separate front doors. It used to be two properties. There's no access between the two premises except by going outside. Even now a buyer will have the option of taking one or both parts."

"Thank you. Now, the two of you. If you hear from your brother, contact the police immediately. This is the number I can be reached on…" he wrote on a page from his notebook and handed it to Mrs Slater. "Or, talk to Chief Inspector Webber at the Westminster Road police station here in the city. Don't on any account try to talk to your brother about this."

"No, we won't. But I suppose when this reaches court, all the stuff about our father will come out in public, and everyone will know. What with the shame of that, and the fact that my brother will be hanged for sure, I think we may have to emigrate or something."

Slater shook his head sadly.

"Isn't there a chance that they'll say he's insane, and send him to Moss Side or somewhere?" asked his wife.

"If we find your brother-in-law and he stands trial, Mrs Slater, I have no doubt that his defending counsel will argue that he is insane. The court works on criteria called the M'Naghten Rules, now nearly a hundred years old. Basically, everyone is presumed to be sane. The defence would have to prove that either he didn't know what he was doing, or if he did know, that he didn't know it was wrong.

"I can't help thinking that the amount of planning that went into all these cases, and the fact that there are so many of them, will make it very difficult to establish either of those options."

Leaving the Slaters, the five policemen had a brief discussion on the pavement. Adair had guessed that a crowd would have gathered, but by some miracle there was nobody visible in the street.

"This isn't working out," he said, briefly outlining what had been learned in the house. "We'll take a look at the shop, but I fear we aren't going to find our man there either."

It was only a five-minute drive to Platt Street. All five officers went first into the living accommodation, and then into the shop. The room immediately behind the shop itself was a workshop, with a number of timepieces on benches. The DCI eyed a bench equipped with a large magnifying lens on a stand, with a wooden-jawed vice behind it.

"Is there a fingerprint kit in your car, Wainwright?" He enquired.

"Yes, sir."

"See what you can find on that lens, and on the vice handle. And there is a nice pointed bradawl tool there too, although I doubt if you'll get any prints off the wooden handle.

"Something on this bench over here, sir,"

called Davison. "Could this be gun oil in this little bottle, and do you think this brush and so on might be a gun cleaning kit?"

"Could very well be," said Adair, "but I think it's possible that watch and clock mechanisms might be cleaned with the same stuff. Still, see if you can get prints off this bottle too, Wainwright.

"Now, I'm going back to Westminster Road. Fleetwood can take me. I want to see what members of the press I can get hold of, and also issue an 'all stations' call for Stephen Slater.

"Wainwright, when you've finished with the prints, return the keys to David Slater, and then take these two back to Preston.

"Sorry you've come all this way for nothing, Pollard. I'll keep the Colt for the time being – I still hope to meet our man in the next day or so.

"Find somewhere to eat on the way, gentlemen. Davison, go straight to the hotel when you get back – I shouldn't be far behind you."

***

Back at the police station, the Scotland Yard DCI found the local DCI waiting for news. It took only five minutes to report the salient points.

"Bad luck, Adair. Poor intelligence from this end regarding that address – apologies."

"Not your fault; it was the address Slater gave. Anyway, I'm after two things. Can you get an 'all stations' call out – certainly all over Lancashire but also London – for Stephen Slater? You know the sort of thing – the police would like to talk to this man urgently – likely to be armed and dangerous – No member of the public to approach him. The contact number had better be that for county HQ. Can you get hold of a mug shot?"

"Sure, but getting that out to stations will take time. I'll get moving on a simple notice. What else?"

"Do you have contact details for local reporters and so on? I want to enlist the help of the Press now."

"Yes. Hang on a minute." Webber opened a book on his desk and flicked through the pages. He quickly wrote down four numbers.

"The Echo and the Daily Star – both Liverpool papers – and the Lancashire Daily Post based in Preston and the Lancashire Evening Telegraph in Blackburn. Those last two cover the area of all four murders. There are lots of other papers, of course, but that'll give you a start. Use my telephone while I go and initiate the notice."

Adair asked for the first number, and spent several minutes before he could speak to a reporter. After identifying himself, he gave a simple statement. He repeated the exercise with the three other newspapers. All agreed to send a reporter to Westminster Road the next morning, to pick up a copy of the photograph.

He then asked the operator to find him the number for Reuters in London. After an even longer delay, he was able to make his statement to that organisation too.

Feeling tired and hungry, he nearly abandoned his task, but decided to get onto the Press Association in London first. As he finished that call, Webber returned.

"All arranged. Calls will go out to Lancashire stations over the next hour, and the Met immediately after."

"OK – many, many thanks. Just to warn you – I've promised the local press boys that if they come here tomorrow they can get a photo."

"That's OK. I'll get a photographer onto making copies as soon as possible."

"Thanks. I want to go. Do you know where my driver is?"

"He's jawing with our Custody Sergeant downstairs. Anytime you need more help, do come back."

The two men shook hands, and Adair went down to find Fleetwood.

"Back to Preston, Constable, and we'll find somewhere to eat on the way."

***

It was after ten o'clock when Fleetwood dropped Adair at the Theatre Hotel. The DCI found Davison drinking a cup of coffee in the residents' lounge, and flopped into an armchair beside him. Waving aside the ministrations of a waiter, he quietly outlined what he had done.

"We were too late for the evening paper

today, of course, and tomorrow's won't have the mug shot – not the first editions anyway. Incidentally, thinking about what the lovelorn Mary Bacon said, I put in the possibility that our man might be wearing a beard.

"Just a question of hoping we get some reports – I don't see that there's anything else to be done at the moment.

"I'm off to bed. Fleetwood will pick us up at eight thirty. I'll see you at breakfast."

CHAPTER 18

On arriving at the county police headquarters, the Desk Sergeant handed the DCI a little pile of papers.

"Five calls for you already, sir. Mr Wainwright left a note for our switchboard operator here last night saying that if there were calls before you gentlemen or he got in, we were to take a message and not try to pass them to anyone else."

"Fine; tell your operator that we are here now, please."

In their room, Adair looked through the notes.

"None of these look useful," he reported. "All are from Liverpool bobbies who know Slater. But nobody is suggesting an address, and all are reporting sightings dating back several weeks."

He pushed the notes aside, and stared into space with a morose expression on his face.

Inspector Wainwright stuck his head in the door, and asked to be excused, as he had received an urgent and unexpected summons to give evidence in Lancaster.

"No, you carry on; there's nothing to do until we get some more intelligence."

"Okay, sir – I've seen the morning paper – perhaps your appeal will bring in something. I'm sorry to desert you."

After Wainwright disappeared, the two officers sat in silence for a quarter of an hour. Then the telephone rang. Davison answered, making notes as he listened to the caller. After a minute, he said "thank you for that, Mrs Bolton; please let us know if you see him again."

"A woman who knows Slater by sight, sir; says she saw him in Platt Street – but that was a fortnight ago."

Adair grunted. "All right. We'll take turns to pick up the 'phone. Me next."

Over the next hour and a half, calls came in at remarkably regular intervals. None provided any useful information. Then, at nearly ten minutes to eleven, Davison took a call which suddenly made him sit up straight.

"Can you say that again madam, please?...Your address?...Yes...When did he move in?...I see, yes...As near as you can say, when did you see that?...Good...Has he been there all the time since he first arrived, or has he been absent at all?...So roughly when did he go?...Yes...Right...Does he have a car or a motor cycle or anything?...When he first arrived, did he mention his employment?...Really?...No, certainly not...

THE NUMBERED MURDERS

Does he see the newspaper?...Good...Where are you now?...Give me the number, if you please... Now, it's essential that you stay exactly where you are...Don't even think of going home...We'll come at once, but it'll take best part of an hour...Tell me about your house...I see; is there access from the back onto another road or what?...Oh, that's ideal...All right, Mrs Baxter, thank you – we'll talk to you again very soon...Goodbye."

Davison turned to his boss.

"This one sounds good, sir. Mrs Baxter is a widow. She lives not half a mile from The Goulds. She has quite a big house, and now lets out a bit of it – a bedroom, living room, bathroom, and a kitchenette – separate from her part of the house, and with a separate entrance.

"About a month ago, she got her first tenant, who answered her advertisement. A young man, early twenties she thinks, with a pronounced Liverpudlian accent. He gave his name as Christopher Holmes. He told her he was a writer, and just wanted somewhere quiet to work and go around doing research.

"Since he arrived he has been away from the house for two or three nights – she can't be more specific.

"He doesn't have a vehicle – at least she's never seen one – but he always seems to have plenty of money, and she knows he's called a taxi a couple of times.

"But when she saw the appeal in the

153

newspaper this morning, what made her call us was this. A week or so ago – again she's vague on dates – she happened to see Holmes leave the house wearing a beard. Now she'd spoken to him the previous evening, and he was clean shaven then. As he was when she next spoke to him a day or so later. She thought it was very odd, as it was obviously false, but it wasn't any of her business and she didn't mention it to him."

"This could be the breakthrough," said Adair happily. "You asked about the house?"

"Yes sir. Good from our point of view. It's detached, standing in about an acre, gardens front and rear. But the back garden has a brick wall on three sides – too high to climb over, Mrs B says. So he has to come out from the front.

"She says he's there now. She is actually on the telephone herself, but when she saw the paper she decided to leave the house and go along to a friend next-door-but-one, and call us from there. She has no idea if he's going out, of course – some days he does, and some days he doesn't. He doesn't have a newspaper delivered, so perhaps he doesn't know about your appeal."

"Right. You go and find Fleetwood. Tell him where we're going, so he can find out how to get to this street. I'm going to get onto Pollard and see whether he or someone else can come armed."

Davison left the room, and Adair picked up the telephone and asked to be put through to Inspector Pollard. Here, he was out of luck – the

Inspector had gone to Lytham, and nobody knew when he would be back. After several questions, the DCI eventually found that Detective Sergeant Ellison was authorised to use firearms, and managed to track the officer down in the mess room.

A few minutes later, Ellison arrived upstairs, and shook hands with Adair.

The DCI gave him a brief outline of the position, although the Sergeant had been with Wainwright at the outset of the Cavanagh case, and had heard some of the later facts from his DI.

"What gun have you drawn?" enquired Adair.

"I saw from the log book that you took a Colt, sir, so I've got the same. I've fired it often enough on the range, but never in anger."

"That makes two of us, Sergeant – and I don't want that situation to change if it can possibly be avoided.

"Now, anticipating that if this goes as we hope we'll need to leave people searching while Slater is brought back here, we'll need another car. Can you find one, Sergeant?"

Ellison said that he had one, and at that moment Davison returned with Fleetwood.

"Right; you take Mr Davison, Sergeant, and I'll travel with Fleetwood. Let's go.

***

Mrs Baxter's house was not far from the

Gould residence, and proved to be of similar size and standing. Fleetwood drove a little past the property, and stopped the car in front of the one next door. Ellison pulled up a few yards further along. All four men got out and stood together on the grass verge.

"Right," said Adair. "Ellison, you and I will walk up the driveway. Have your hand on your gun, but don't draw it until I say. Davison, you and Fleetwood wait until we are almost at the house before following. We'll go round to Slater's door at the side. I'll knock, and assuming he is in we'll try to take him. It seems unlikely that he'll come to the door with a drawn pistol.

"If he isn't in we'll have to retire to the car and think again. Come on, Ellison."

The two officers, each with a hand in a pocket, walked the short distance along the road and turned in through the open gates. They were only a few yards inside the property when the DCI's plan was disrupted.

A man appeared from the side of the house. He didn't see the detectives at first, walking along the frontage, but he spotted them as soon as he turned right towards the gate. Some instinct told him these were policemen.

Immediately, his hand went to his own pocket, and came out holding a gun.

"Draw," snapped Adair, and both officers started to pull out their own automatics.

Slater fired once before they could do the

same, and they heard the bullet thwack into the gatepost just behind them.

"Wait," ordered Adair, each officer now down on one knee with both hands on his gun in the classic pose. "Fire if he raises the gun towards us again. Shoot to kill."

Slater seemed to hesitate when he saw the two guns trained on him unwaveringly, only twenty yards away, and stood still, the arm with the revolver now down at his side.

Still glaring at the two officers, and now also at the two others he could see not far behind them, he started to shout and swear loudly. After a few seconds of this, he yelled:

"They shot my dad; they're not going to hang me!"

With that, he quickly placed the muzzle of the revolver in his mouth, and changed his grip so that his thumb rather than his forefinger was now on the trigger.

Immediately after that, he squeezed the trigger.

There was an audible 'click', as the hammer fell.

Slater seemed not to realise what had happened, and made no attempt to fire again.

While he just stood there, apparently in shock, Adair and Ellison jumped up and were on to him in seconds, quickly pocketing their own pistols. Ellison, a foot taller than Adair and fleeter of foot, arrived a yard ahead. He quickly grabbed the revolver and pulled it out of Slater's mouth. The other two policemen joined them, and Fleetwood produced a set of handcuffs with which he secured the still shaking man.

"Search him, Constable," directed the DCI.

This produced a key (evidently for the house door), a wallet containing over fifteen pounds, and a handful of loose change.

Ellison broke the revolver, and checked it.

"Only the one dud round here plus the cartridge of the shot he just fired. I reckon when he found the gun it only had the six bullets, sir."

"Looks like it," agreed Adair. "And I suppose after over twenty years one dud out of six isn't bad.

"Right. You have the privilege of arresting him, Sergeant. Unlawful possession of a firearm, and for attempting to murder a police officer. Those would do to hold him, but you might as well throw in suspicion of the murders of Aidan Cavanagh, Paul Hargreaves, Frank Gould, and Benedict Foster-Nash, as well."

Ellison smiled, and proceeded to carry out the formal arrest.

"Tell him his rights, Fleetwood," added the Sergeant, "although it doesn't look as though he's taking much in at present."

"Good," said Adair when this was all done. "Take him to Sergeant Ellison's car, Constable, and sit in the back with him. Leave your car key with me.

"Sergeant, I think his bullet hit that gatepost

– see if you can dig it out. It might be useful. Then you drive Slater back and get him booked in. And make sure that duff cartridge is stored safely.

"Davison, take the house key and start searching Slater's rooms. I'll go and talk to Mrs Baxter, and then come to join you."

Adair walked along the road to the house where Mrs Baxter had taken refuge. At the gate of this property stood two ladies in late middle age, and indeed there were several other little gatherings along the road, people obviously deciding that after the single shot it was now safe to emerge and find out what was going on.

The DCI identified himself to the ladies, and learned which was Mrs Baxter.

"Shall we go back to your house, ma'am? It's quite safe now, and I'll need a statement."

"I wonder if you would do me a favour," he said to Mrs Baxter's friend. "I don't have time to explain to the onlookers what's happened, but they have a right to know what the shooting was about.

"Please tell everyone that, thanks to Mrs Baxter here, we have taken a man into custody. He is a suspect in the four murder cases you've probably read about in the newspapers. The suspect fired one shot this morning, as everyone no doubt heard. The police were armed, but did not return fire. Nobody has been hurt. That's all I can say – thank you."

He escorted Mrs Baxter back to her house.

"As you've gathered, ma'am, the man who said his name was Holmes is, we believe, Stephen Slater. Anyway, you've helped us enormously, and there is no longer any danger here."

At the front door, he explained that he was going to see his colleague in the annexe, and would return shortly to discuss a statement. The lady immediately offered to give both men some lunch.

"I have a large piece of pork pie, Chief Inspector, and some cold potatoes. It was going to be two meals for me, but it might just about feed the two of you. There's also plenty of bread and butter."

"Very kind, ma'am, but we mustn't deprive you, and we need to get away as soon as possible anyway. Perhaps a cup of tea or coffee while I take your statement?"

An hour later, Mrs Baxter had signed her statement, and Davison had collected a cardboard box (provided by Mrs B) full of papers from Slater's rooms.

"Plenty of proof that he's been actively researching both his father's case and the four dead men," explained the DI. "There's also stuff on the man he didn't get to."

"Excellent; as good as we could have hoped for," replied Adair.

"I assume all the furniture and so on is yours?" Adair asked Mrs Baxter, as he and his colleague were preparing to leave.

"That's right, Chief Inspector. Will I be able

to re-let the place soon? I'll be a lot more choosy about a tenant next time!"

"The next of kin is a twin brother – a very decent man. I'll talk to him, but I'll be astounded if he even wants to claim the clothing and so on. If he doesn't, and I'll let you know in a couple of days, then I suggest that you clear all Slater's stuff out – or get someone else to do it – and then dump it in your garage or shed. Keep it for a month, and then dispose of it. Slater will either hang or spend the rest of his life inside.

"As soon as you've cleared the rooms, you can re-let as far as the police are concerned."

The two officers called at a roadside inn on the way back to Preston, where they had lunch. Both wished they had accepted Mrs Baxter's offer!

CHAPTER 19

Back at the station, Adair and Davison found Ellison talking to the Custody Sergeant.

"Slater asked for a mouthpiece, sir, almost as soon as we got back," reported the DS. "We found him Russell Bagnall, who arrived a few minutes ago. He's with his client now. There's a constable outside the interview room."

"Did he say anything else on the journey?" asked Davison.

"Not much that is printable, sir, and certainly nothing usable. I've come across people with chips on their shoulders – well this one has an oak tree."

The Yard detectives grinned.

"What's Bagnall like, Sergeant?" enquired Davison.

"Not a bad type, as defence lawyers go. Quite young, but doesn't go around shouting his mouth off all the time. 'Realistic' would be a fair description, sir. But he'll certainly do his best for every client."

"We'll give them half an hour," said Adair.

"Let's all go up to the office, and we can see about statements. I also need to make some telephone calls, but I think I'll leave those until we've seen Slater."

The three men sat drafting their statements. All were experienced at this task, and there was little conversation for the next forty minutes.

Adair put down his pen and was about to speak when the telephone rang. He picked it up.

"Yes?...Right...No, I think not. I don't know how big your interview rooms are but I bet there isn't room for five people in any sort of comfort. We'll do it up here instead. Send Mr Bagnall up first. Give us ten minutes with him, and then have Slater brought up here too.

"Bagnall is ready, gentlemen. Any bets on how this'll go?"

"A 'no comment' interview, probably," opined Davison.

"Agreed," said Ellison, "but not silent – there'll be a lot of bad language."

Adair didn't give his own opinion, and Davison, who knew very well that despite the way the question had been put, his boss never bet, nevertheless asked where he was going to put his own money.

The DCI grinned, aware that this was a gentle dig.

"I'm expecting a full confession, gentlemen – probably made completely contrary to his lawyer's advice."

There was a tap on the door, and a constable showed the smartly-suited young Solicitor into the room.

Ellison performed the introductions, and after the usual round of handshaking, the four men sat down again.

The policemen all looked at Bagnall, who smiled faintly.

"My client is prepared to be questioned, gentlemen. I make clear that I have advised him to remain absolutely silent, but he has rejected that advice.

"As we go along, it is likely that I will advise him not to answer various questions – but it seems probable that he will again ignore that advice.

"However, as he must be clinically insane, I don't know that it matters greatly. In due course I think he will be found unfit to plead."

Davison and Ellison looked at the DCI to see how he would respond, but he just looked expressionlessly at the lawyer and said nothing.

"Your Custody Sergeant told me the reasons for his arrest. Regarding the first two matters, my client has not said anything about what happened today, although I gather it was traumatic for him. I know nothing about the suspicion of murder matters apart from what I read in the newspapers."

"What happened this morning, Mr Bagnall, is that your client fired a shot from a revolver at the police officers approaching him. Two of us were armed, but we did not fire back. Your client then said 'they shot my father but they aren't going to hang me'. He then placed the muzzle of his gun in his mouth and pulled the trigger. The gun contained a defective round, and failed to fire. I daresay that, having decided to take his own life and actually pulled the trigger, to then find he was still alive might well have been something of a shock.

"We could charge your client with the two offences – even with attempting to commit suicide, but of course none of those will be preferred. We'll talk about the other allegations in a minute."

The Solicitor didn't reply, but looked worried.

Seconds later, Slater was brought in. He was led to the chair next to Bagnall, and Adair told the escorting constable to remove the handcuffs and then wait outside the door.

Davison and Ellison took out pencils and got ready to make notes.

"Now, Slater," began the DCI, "you've been told you don't have to say anything, but that anything you do say may be taken down and used in evidence.

"Let's start with this morning. Why did you pull out a gun and shoot at us?"

"Obvious. You were going to arrest me."

"Very true. Where did you get the revolver?"

"I found it in a cupboard in my stepfather's workshop after he died."

"Did you find any ammunition with it?"

"Only the bullets what was loaded in it."

"Why did you scratch a number on each one?"

"Dunno, really. I'd been finding out who was involved in killing my dad, and I knew there was five of them left. There were generals involved too, but they're dead already. And there were four witnesses, but they all died later in the war.

"When I found the gun I knew God had given me the means to get even with the others. I just scratched the numbers on, so I could keep score, I suppose.

"The Solicitor here thinks I'm mad – putting the numbers on must help to prove it."

"The five men, Slater. Tell us about them."

"I advise you to say nothing more," interjected Bagnall.

Slater waved this aside. "No bloody point," he growled. "Do shut up. I didn't manage to shoot myself, so they'll lock me up in Moss Side or that other place, Broadmoor.

"I found who was involved in dad's trial. The three officers on what they called the court. The one who ran the prosecution. And the one who was supposed to be my dad's 'friend' but did nothing to save him.

"My only regret is that I only got two of the judges."

Bagnall shook his head sadly.

"Tell us about the girl, Mary Bacon – Colonel

Gould's maid."

"She was useful. Told me stuff about the household, so I could fix for getting one woman out of the way and getting the job done when the others were out. She liked me, I think, but I'm not much interested in having a regular girl."

"After each man was shot, why did you take the cartridge out of the revolver and put it on or beside the body?"

"Again, dunno really. Just seemed right somehow. So Cavanagh. When I took his shell case and laid it on his chest, I just thought 'this is the first, and I had the number there to show it. Then number two for Hargreaves, and so on."

"Why did you want to get revenge in the first place?"

"Obvious again. Dad was a good man. Killing him deprived me of a proper father, and condemned me to a horrible life."

Adair looked at Slater coldly.

Davison, who had seen the DCI tear into suspects before and had been surprised when he hadn't said anything to the Solicitor earlier, waited expectantly. He wasn't disappointed.

"What a load of utter codswallop, Slater. In the first place, your father was not a 'good man'. He'd been in prison twice before he even went into the army, and if his previous conduct while in the army hadn't been so poor he might have had his death sentence commuted – the vast majority of others in that position did.

"Then your mother married a really decent man, who'd been awarded medals for bravery and so on. You were given a good stepfather – one who was a far better role model than your real one could ever have been.

"And if you were condemned to this 'terrible life', how come your twin brother, with exactly the same heredity and environment, has turned out so well. He holds down a respectable job, and has married a very nice girl – and he has never been in court for offences of dishonesty and violence as you so often have. The plain fact is you're just a nasty piece of work."

"Really, Chief Inspector," protested Bagnall, "you shouldn't talk to my client like that. He's innocent until proved guilty, and you're treating him like a common criminal."

"Come on, Mr Bagnall; your client stands condemned out of his own mouth. Anyway, he's been a common criminal for years."

All three detectives had been expecting a tirade of foul language – especially Ellison, who had heard Slater's expletive-ridden rant in the car earlier. Now, suddenly, the man did indeed let loose another volley of bad language. This was not, perhaps surprisingly, aimed in any way at Adair, but generally at the system which he kept repeating had wrongly convicted his father. It went on for over a minute.

"Do you agree with your mouthpiece about your sanity?" asked Adair in a conversational tone, when the rant stopped.

"About the only thing where I do agree with him. Stands to reason I'm mad. Wouldn't have killed all these people, otherwise. Wouldn't have tried to kill myself either. Oh, I'm a lunatic all right."

"More rubbish," replied Adair. "The detailed research and planning you put into this scheme – you knew exactly what you were doing all the way along."

"Ah, but he didn't know that what he was doing was wrong," insisted Bagnall.

"Really? The jury will never buy that one. Lots of little things will prove that he did know. Giving a false name to Mary Bacon, and disguising himself with a false beard so she couldn't identify him. Giving a different false name to Mrs Baxter when he took rooms with her. And I think when we go through his papers we'll find that he gave more false names when researching the details of the court-martial. People don't need to disguise themselves and give false names if they don't think they're doing anything wrong.

"I'm not a betting man, Mr Bagnall, but if I were I'd put every penny I'd got on the trial ending with a death sentence for your client – with no possibility of a reprieve.

"Stephen Slater, I charge you with the murders of Aiden Cavanagh, Paul Hargreaves, Benedict Foster-Nash, and Frank Gould, contrary to the Common Law. The dates and places will be added to the indictment.

"We'll put you in front of a magistrate in the morning.

"Do you want to talk to your client any more?" he asked Bagnall.

"Not at the moment – I need to start looking for counsel – and for a medical opinion."

"Constable!" shouted Adair.

The man opened the door and stuck his head inside the room.

"Cuff Slater again, and put him in a cell.

To the surprise of everyone, including Bagnall, Slater said absolutely nothing as he was led away.

"Off the record, Chief Inspector," said the Solicitor after Slater had gone, "I wouldn't bet against you on this one. I fear he'll hang."

****

BOOKS BY THIS AUTHOR

The Bedroom Window Murder

Book 1 in the Philip Bryce series, set in 1949.

The Courthouse Murder

Book 2 in the Philip Bryce series.

The Felixstowe Murder

Book 3 in the Philip Bryce series.

Multiples Of Murder

Book 4 in the Philip Bryce series.

Death At Mistram Manor

Book 5 in the Philip Bryce series.

Machinations Of A Murderer

Book 6 in the Philip Bryce series.

Suspicions Of A Parlourmaid And The Norfolk Railway Murders

Book 7 in the Philip Bryce series.

This Village Is Cursed

Book 8 in the Philip Bryce series.

The Amateur Detective

Book 9 in the Philip Bryce series.

Demands With Menaces

Book 10 in the Philip Bryce series.

Murder In Academe

Book 11 in the Philip Bryce series.

Death Of A Safebreaker

A 1936 murder mystery. (Not part of a series)

Death Of A Juror

A 1936 murder mystery. (Not part of a series.)

The Failed Lawyer

A 1952 murder story about a short period in the life of a young man. (Not part of a series.)

Murder In The Rabid Dog

Book 12 in the Philip Bryce series.

The Missing Schoolgirls

A detective mystery, set in 1938,
Book 1 in the David Adair series.

The King's Bench Walk Murder And Death In The Boardroom

Book 13 in the Philip Bryce series.

The Devon Murders

Book 14 in the Philip Bryce series.

Death In Piccadilly

Book 3 in the David Adair series.

Printed in Great Britain
by Amazon